'You want to go to bed with me.'

Jenna had hit on the truth, and he did not like it, but could not deny it; Daniel had done enough deceiving. 'Yes.' His eyes were fierce.

'No strings attached, of course. Just a. . .' she paused to lend emphasis to her words, then said, her voice bitter '. . .a fling.' Her eyes narrowed with contempt. 'You're no better than your brother!'

Dear Reader,

This month Caroline Anderson begins a trilogy detailing the loves of three women who work with children and babies at the Audley Memorial Hospital. PLAYING THE JOKER opens with Jo, whose traumatic past she must keep from Alex—a deeply emotional read. Margaret Barker takes us to Bali, while James plans to snare Marnie in SURGEON'S STRATEGY by Drusilla Douglas, and Jenna Reid finds her looks deny her the man she wants in Patricia Robertson's HEART IN JEOPARDY.

Enjoy!

The Editor

Patricia Robertson has nursed in hospitals, in District Health, and abroad. Now retired, she is incorporating this past experience in her Medical Romances. Widowed with two daughters, she spends her time gardening, reading and taking care of her Yorkshire Terriers. She lives in Scotland.

Recent titles by the same author:

YESTERDAY'S MEMORY
DOCTOR TO THE RESCUE

HEART IN JEOPARDY

BY

PATRICIA ROBERTSON

MILLS & BOON LIMITED
ETON HOUSE   18–24 PARADISE ROAD
RICHMOND   SURREY   TW9 1SR

First published in Great Britain 1992
by Mills & Boon Limited

© Patricia Robertson 1992

Australian copyright 1992
Philippine copyright 1992
This edition 1992

ISBN 0 263 77950 5

Set in 10 on 11 pt Linotron Plantin
03-9212-57925

Typeset in Great Britain by Centracet, Cambridge
Made and printed in Great Britain

CHAPTER ONE

'Who's that?' Jenna's dark brown eyes widened and her heart leapt. It was such an unusual sensation—her raised eyebrows were partly due to surprise. No man had ever roused more than an occasional extra beat in her pulse before.

District Nursing Sister Penelope Brown was sitting at the table. She looked out of the window overlooking Bellingham Health Centre's car park to where Jenna was pointing.

'That,' she said with a sigh, 'is the admirable Dr White.'

The tall blond man's face was in profile. His jaw was square, his nose straight. You could not see the colour of his eyes, but Penny knew they were blue, a lovely heavenly blue. She sighed again.

'Isn't he gorgeous?' She was lost in a fantasy world where there were no sick people, only handsome blond men who all looked like Daniel White.

'He's certainly good to look at,' agreed Jenna, who could not drag her eyes away from the athletic figure striding towards the entrance. Even his back was attractive in its well-fitting grey suit. She felt almost bereft when he vanished as the doors closed behind him, and laughed. How fanciful can you get? she thought.

Penny glanced across the table at her friend.

'What's the joke?' she asked.

'Nothing really.' Jenna smiled, and the smile lit the sombreness of her features, putting life into the dark, almost black eyes. Her full lips needed no make-up and the olive skin was smooth and unblemished. The dark hair, the colour of her eyes, was chin-length and curly; wisps of it fell across her high broad cheekbones.

'Do you have any Italian blood in your veins?' Penny asked, not for the first time.

Jenna's big mouth widened as she laughed. 'Oh, Penny!' She shook her head from side to side, her hair swinging. 'You know I have. My grandfather.'

Penny sighed. 'Yes—sorry. It's just not fair that you should look like that—sexy, alluring, while some of us. . .' She grinned, not really envious of her friend. She herself was petite and pretty. She also knew the price such as her friend's looks exacted, knew how Jenna had been sexually harassed in the past.

'I'm glad you accepted this post.' She grinned again.

'I wouldn't be here,' admitted Jenna, 'if that ghastly registrar at our training hospital hadn't driven me to take the district nursing training. I hope to escape such unwelcome advances in this field of work.' Sombreness came back into her dark eyes.

'You'll be happy here,' said Penny cheerfully. 'Daniel White is a marvellous doctor.' Admiration filled her blue eyes. 'He's devoted to his work and doesn't play around, more's the pity.' She grimaced regretfully.

Jenna laughed. 'What a shame!' But she found her friend's words hard to believe. It was Jenna's experience that every man, handsome or not, devoted to his work or not, was sexually motivated.

The door opening prevented further conversation. A woman, large of face and figure, came in. Her blue uniform was creased from sitting in the car, and there was a sheen of perspiration on her face. She dropped her black nursing bag on to the table.

'Glad I didn't put on my mac,' she said, a smile lighting her blue eyes, creasing their corners. 'It's going to be hot.'

Jenna had automatically stood up—the grey-haired nurse had a presence that commanded respect.

'You must be Jenna Reid.' The older woman came forward, hand outstretched. 'You're taking over from me.' A sudden sadness aged her face. 'Can't say I'll be sorry to retire.' But the sadness belied her words. 'I'm Muriel Thomas.'

The hand in Jenna's felt damp.

'Let's see,' Muriel frowned, 'this is Wednesday, and I finish for good on Friday.' She smiled. 'That should give me time enough to show you the ropes.'

Jenna thought she detected doubt in the retiring nurse's eyes, doubt as to whether her replacement was capable, but Jenna was not dismayed. She had seen it so often before. In fact, she came to expect it when she took up a new post. She could read the faces of new colleagues and knew they were wondering if anyone with the face and figure of a sex symbol could be a serious nurse. They were convinced she was only out to catch a man, probably their husband, their consultant or their favourite doctor. Jenna was surprised, therefore, when Muriel did not say, 'Of course Dr White will be immune to your charms,' as Jenna had heard so often before.

'The patients are going to be spoilt, having two pretty nurses attending to them now.' Muriel Thomas's eyes were kind as she looked at Jenna. 'I'll show you over the Health Centre when we come back for coffee.' Muriel glanced at her watch. 'I gave two of the diabetics their insulin on my way in, but I left Mrs Ledson so that you could meet her.' Muriel smiled. 'She's a darling, but a bit absentminded.'

Penny grinned. 'She's a real sweetie.'

The nurses' room was square, with a filing cabinet in one corner and two large cupboards along the wall. Muriel opened the drawer of the large table at which Penny was seated and from which Jenna had seen the handsome doctor, and drew out a key. Crossing to one of the cupboards, she unlocked it and threw back the doors, rather too briskly, so that they swung back, almost hitting her.

'I'm sure this cupboard doesn't like me,' she said.

Penny laughed, and Jenna smiled. The incident relieved the tension she was feeling.

Syringes followed by needles, dressing packs, sachets of lotion, sterile scissors, all pre-packed, piled on to the table. 'Do you want anything?' Muriel glanced at Penny.

The blonde nurse raised her head from the list she was making. 'Stitch-removing pack, please.'

Muriel put it beside her. Then, drawing a navy blue bag from her pocket, she pushed dressing packs, syringes, needles and anything else she needed into it.

'Ready to go?' she said to Jenna.

Jenna was already on her feet. She had deliberately asked for a size larger dress than her usual twelve in the hope it would disguise her thirty-eight-inch chest. It did to some extent, but the top pockets, one on either side for pens, emphasised her figure rather than hid it. The blue of her uniform suited her dark colouring and made her look more exotic. Even the red geraniums on the windowsills lost some of their colour by comparison.

'Can I take that?' Jenna gestured towards the blue bag.

'Thanks.' Muriel handed it to her, lifting her nurse's bag with the other hand. 'You coming?' She glanced towards Penny.

'In a minute.' The fair girl did not look up; she was still sorting her workload. 'Don't wait for me.'

Jenna had her hand stretched towards the door-handle when the door opened suddenly, after a perfunctory knock, and Daniel White followed too quickly for Jenna to step aside, so that they were face to face, inches apart.

His impact on her was immense. Her whole body leapt into life. His profile had been handsome, but in full face the effect was devastating, and when he smiled she was undone. She felt as if she were drowning in his blue eyes. His teeth were even whiter because of his tan, and his hair had been bleached lighter by the sun. The lines on his brow and beside his mouth did not detract from his handsomeness, rather they added a maturity to it. But there was a reserve about the face which his smile did not lift.

Jenna could not have been more shocked at the effect he had on her than if he had struck her. Indeed, she was stricken. She had fallen in love immediately, completely and overwhelmingly. She staggered slightly, and a hand reached forward to grasp her arm. It was a strong hand, but she knew instinctively that it could be gentle. His fingers seemed to burn on her skin, and she jerked back.

'I'm sorry,' he said. Jenna knew his voice would be deep. 'Did I hurt you?' His concern warmed her.

Just my heart, she would have liked to have said, and the sudden picture of an arrow through that heart broke the tension of his touch and she smiled, more at herself than at him.

'No—it was just the suddenness.' Her love for him made her voice sound low, provocative, quite unintentionally.

Daniel White's eyes narrowed. He felt the pull of her, felt an instant attraction, and did not welcome it.

'Good.' His voice was brisk, all concern for her vanished.

Jenna was astonished at the rebuff. Normally, men fell at her feet, some literally, but this man was untouched. The one time she would have welcomed open admiration it was not forthcoming.

She stepped aside, her sudden ardour dampened, and let him pass, but as he passed his sleeve brushed her arm and she suppressed a small gasp.

'I wanted to catch you before you left.' He was smiling at Muriel, whose eyes lit with affection as she looked at him.

Jenna was visualising the delights that lay ahead,

delights that filled her with excitement. She had never felt so alive. Confidence in her sexuality and the knowledge of how attractive she was made it unthinkable that Daniel White would be immune to her for long, so she was not disheartened by his rebuff.

'I hope you haven't been to Mrs Ledson yet?' Daniel's eyebrows rose enquiringly, and, when Muriel replied in the negative, he said, 'Good. Would you tell her I've arranged an outpatient appointment for her at Swansford General on the twenty-third of July?' A resigned expression crossed his face. 'It's at eleven a.m. Please impress on her to go this time.'

Muriel smiled. 'I'll do my best, Daniel, but. . .' She spread her hands and shrugged.

Daniel grinned. What a gorgeous smile! mused Jenna, almost drooling. Then, catching sight of the astonished expression on Penny's face as her friend looked at her, she composed her own.

'That's fair enough,' said Daniel, and turned to leave.

Jenna had moved so that she would be out of Penny's sight, and in doing so, was behind Daniel. As he turned he was almost touching her again.

Damn the girl, he thought, as they did a dodge about to avoid each other. He had his hand on the door-handle when Muriel said,

'Oh, Daniel, I'd like to introduce you to the nurse who's taking over from me—Jenna Reid.' She gestured towards her replacement.

Daniel turned, trying as he did so to fix his face into a pleasant smile. The lips succeeded, but the eyes didn't. They looked almost hostile.

'How do you do?' he said, his hand reaching forward in an involuntary gesture of friendship, one which he did not feel.

Jenna was undismayed. She smiled, and the smile was confident, as were the eyes. Her hand was cool and slim in his larger one, but its delicateness was not a sign that this nurse was timid or shy, he decided. No, this woman—she must be about twenty-six, he guessed— did not need protection, quite the reverse. It was the men she came into contact with who commanded his sympathy. She was no Elaine, who was serene in her beauty, not voluptuous and provocative as this nurse was.

The veiled hostility became positive dislike, and this did disturb Jenna. For the first time in her life she felt unsure—unable to speak, and just inclined her head in recognition of the introduction.

'I hope you'll be happy here.' The words fell hollowly from Daniel's lips and he wished he had not said them.

Jenna's sense of humour asserted itself as she saw his discomfort at the lie and she could not resist saying,

'Thank you, Doctor. I'm sure I shall be.' There was laughter in her eyes.

Damn the girl—no, woman, he corrected. She's laughing at me. And this time *he* was disconcerted and uncomfortable.

Jenna, opening the door for him and inclining her head, was a further aggravation, and he swept out quite pompously.

'Come on,' said Muriel, 'let's go.'

Penny was now ready to join them and locked the door behind them.

'We leave the key in Reception,' she told her friend. 'I'll show you where on our way out.'

The building was only two years old, single-storeyed. They went down a corridor, and Jenna noticed Daniel's name on one of the doctors' doors. At the end was a large waiting-room and the reception area, which was quite large and set out rather like a bank, half-counter and half-glass. The patients' case-notes were contained in two circular tiers resembling bastions.

Penny had introduced Jenna to the two receptionists when they had arrived. Linda Shaw was a middle-aged woman with dyed blonde hair. She was as tall as Jenna's five foot seven. Her slightly harassed air was reflected in her hurried expression—frown to laughter, laughter to frown. Shirley Gardener was a sensible-looking woman of about thirty, with a thoughtful expression and kind eyes. Her slimness made her appear taller than her five foot three.

'Any messages?' Muriel asked as Penny hung up the key.

'Mrs Dickens was on the line. Said you missed her bath yesterday,' Linda said, worry lines deepening on her forehead.

'Well, really!' An aggravated frown drew Muriel's eyebrows together. 'I told her daughter on the phone yesterday that I'd have to change her mother's bath day to today. I suppose she must have forgotten to tell her mother.' Muriel sighed. 'Thanks anyway.'

The car was hot when they stepped into it, and Jenna wished she could have left her tights off.

'See you about eleven!' called Penny as Muriel wound down the car's window.

Muriel nodded.

'Do you have a car?' asked the older nurse as they clicked on their seatbelts.

'Yes,' said Jenna. 'A Mini, like Penny's, but I left it at Penny's and came in with her.'

'Oh, yes.' Muriel stopped the car at the entrance to the Health Centre's car park and looked up and down the road. 'I remember now. She told me you were sharing her flat.' When the road was clear she swung left and joined the heavy traffic. 'I won't be sorry to miss this,' she said, nodding at the cars. 'Even the dual carriageway is busy at eight-thirty. All the commuters come in from the villages around Swansford. When I came here years ago there were just fields here. Now look at it!' She gestured to the council houses on one side of Bellingham Road and to the high-rise blocks on the other. 'At least they're renovating the flats at last. You should have seen them before—facing fallen off, graffiti everywhere!'

Jenna thought the flats looked quite cheerful with their different-coloured patches, and said so.

'Don't be misled.' Muriel's tone was grim. 'The paint covers a great deal of misery.'

They rounded a roundabout and returned up the opposite side of the road. Jenna glanced past Muriel towards the Health Centre. It blended with the surrounding buildings, being modern in design. The only difference between it and the high-rise blocks in between which it nestled was in the colour of its bricks—they were red.

Jenna wondered what Daniel was doing now, and, as if her thoughts had been read, Muriel said,

'We're lucky with our doctors. Daniel White's a gem, and his brother, Richard, is almost as good.'

Jenna thought she detected a slight reservation in the older nurse's tone as she mentioned Richard White.

'Penny said the Health Centre catered for two other group practices as well,' Jenna said, deciding to judge Richard White for herself.

'Yes.' Muriel turned left at the next intersection. It was as if they had entered another town, where no high-rise flats raised their coloured heads to the sky. The road was lined with bungalows, all designed alike, with a bay-windowed lounge on one side of the front door and a flat-windowed room on the other.

Muriel turned into the drive of number twenty-eight. Taking her bag from the back seat, they left the car and rang the bell.

'You need to wait—Mrs Ledson takes some time to answer,' she explained.

'Is that you, Nurse?' The unopened door muffled the voice.

'Yes, Mrs Ledson, it's Nurse Thomas.'

The door swung back, some of the green paint flaking away as it did so. A woman of medium height in her early sixties, round of figure with grey hair permed in an old-fashioned style, smiled a greeting.

'I've brought another nurse with me today, Mrs Ledson,' Muriel told her. 'My replacement, Jenna Reid.'

'No one can replace you, Nurse Thomas,' said Mrs Ledson. 'But I'm sure Nurse Reid will be just as good.' And she smiled at Jenna. 'I hope you don't mind my not calling you by your Christian name, Nurse, but I wouldn't feel comfortable.' She waved a deprecating hand. 'You'll have to blame my generation for that—we were always brought up to respect nurses and doctors.'

Mrs Ledson was leading them into the kitchen as she spoke. Reaching up, she opened one of the cupboards and drew out a box. 'I keep all my stuff for the nurse in here.' She looked at Jenna proudly, then took out the bottle of insulin, medi-swabs and a packet of diabetic syringes, picking needles out at the same time. 'Nurse Thomas tried to teach me to give it to myself, but I was too nervous.' Her tone was aploogetic. Then her face brightened. 'But I do manage to test my own urine, and it's blue today.'

Muriel smiled. 'Good. Did you keep a specimen for me to take to the surgery?' She was drawing up the insulin, having checked the dose with the book first in which it was recorded and signed by all the nurses who attended the patient.

Mrs Ledson's hand flew to her mouth. 'Oh, I forgot!' Her eyes were distressed, and Jenna put her arm about the older woman's shoulders.

Muriel gave the dark nurse a smile of approval and said, 'That's all right. I'll put a note with your urine-testing outfit to remind you.' She fitted the orange needle to the syringe and gave the injection. 'You are keeping to your diet, Mrs Ledson?' Muriel asked gently.

'Yes.' Mrs Ledson's tone was anxious. 'My urine test wouldn't be blue otherwise, would it?'

Muriel put her arm round the tense shoulders. There was a similarity between the two women which Jenna could not place immediately—then it came to her. They were of a generation past. They had been brought up in a gentler, more innocent time.

Mrs Ledson packed the insulin and equipment away and put the box at the back of the cupboard. Everything about the kitchen and the hall through which they had passed reflected the tidiness of the owner.

Muriel looked up from the note she was writing to remind the patient to save a specimen of urine for her.

'Dr Daniel asked me to tell you that he's made an outpatients appointment for you on the twenty-third of July at eleven in the morning for the diabetic clinic at Swansford General. Will your son be able to take you?'

Mrs Ledson's lips trembled. 'It's very good of Dr Daniel,' she said. 'He's so kind, but John's in America.' The rims of her eyes reddened. 'He went yesterday to take up that post at the university that I told you about. His family will follow shortly.'

'Oh, yes.' Muriel frowned. 'I'm sorry, I forgot. Could your daughter-in-law take you?'

'I couldn't ask her!' Mrs Ledson's face was aghast. 'She's too busy. What with the children. . .' She turned to Jenna. 'Alan's twelve and Jean's fourteen.' Her expression softened. 'Such lovely children!' There was pride in the way that she spoke. 'And then there's the packing—it would be too much for her. No, I'll just get a taxi.'

'You missed the last appointment like that.' Muriel's tone was firm.

Mrs Ledson lowered her eyes guiltily.

'I know what we can do.' The worry frown left Muriel's brow. 'I'll take you. I'll be a free agent then.'

'Oh, would you?' Tears of relief filled Mrs Ledson's

eyes. Then she frowned. 'But I couldn't let you. You'll
need a rest.'

'I'll have had plenty of rest by then.' Muriel smiled.
'Anyway, I'd like to.' And she pressed Mrs Ledson's
hand.

When they were at the front door, Mrs Ledson said,
'I will see you tomorrow, though, Nurse Thomas, won't
I?'

'You'll see both of us,' Muriel replied, with a smile.

'Double ration of good fortune!' Mrs Ledson's face
relaxed into a smile.

As they drove towards the next case Muriel said,

'It's difficult not to become involved with your
patients on the district. It's not like being in hospital
where you have the patients for a week or two and then
they go home. I've known Mrs Ledson for years. I've
seen her son grow up. I know her family history as well
as my own.' She paused at a pedestrian crossing. 'I
nursed her husband when he had a stroke and I was
there when he died.' She glanced at Jenna with thoughtful eyes. 'You have to be very sure when you take on
this job that you're going to be committed.' She gave
Jenna a sharp look.

The pedestrian way was clear and she moved off.
'And you have to decide just how much you're going to
become involved. It can drain you emotionally. The
trick is to leave your work behind when you go home,
otherwise you'll have nothing left to give to your family.'

They had left the better houses behind and were once
more amongst the high-rise flats. 'We'll bath Mr
Robinson next,' Muriel said briskly. 'He's an asthmatic
and inclined to become agitated if we're late.'

She parked her Metro in one of the spaces provided.
She lifted her bag and checked that she had not left
anything on the back seat. 'You have to be careful,' she
told Jenna. 'Don't leave anything on view—one of the
girls had her car broken into last week.'

They went into the building, adjusting their eyes to the darkened interior. Graffiti marked the wall, and the door through to the back hung on its hinges.

'I hope the lift's working,' said Muriel. 'Mr Robinson lives on the twelfth floor.'

Fortunately they did not have to walk up the stairs, though Jenna almost wished they had had to, for the lift creaked alarmingly and she was glad when they stepped from it.

The flats were entered from a balcony which ran the length of one side. 'At least he gets plenty of air up here,' Muriel said as she rang the bell.

It was a moment or two before the door opened, and when it did Mrs Robinson, a small spare woman with thinning grey hair and a worried expression, said,

'I thought it was Dr Daniel.' Disappointment made her voice sharp.

'Oh!' Immediately both nurses were alert. 'What's wrong?' asked Muriel.

'It's Harry,' Mrs Robinson said over her shoulder as she went before them. 'He's having an attack!'

Muriel and Jenna followed her down the hall, and Jenna could not help but notice how different it was from Mrs Ledson's. Hand-prints made a smudged design on the cream emulsion and the floor was covered with vinyl, worn down to the boards in places. An overall stale smell compounded of cooking and dogs hung in the atmosphere.

A thud against a door they were passing made Jenna jump.

'It's only Ben, Nurse,' said Mrs Robinson. 'We have to shut him up when Dr Daniel and the nurse come, otherwise they'd be licked to death!' A strained smile crossed her face and Jenna grinned. 'I've left the front door unlocked for Dr Daniel. He should be here in a minute.'

They entered the lounge, which was a through room.

A window overlooked the countryside at the back. Jenna had not realised how far out from the town centre this estate was. The contrast between the ordered farmland sheltered by trees whose leaves shone brightly in the sunshine and the meanness of the lounge they were in struck her forcibly and roused her compassion.

But such thoughts left her as quickly as they had come when she saw the patient looking as worn and threadbare as the chair he was sitting in. She hurried forward, oblivious to everything, her whole being concentrated on relieving the patient, whose breathing was stressed and whose skin was grey and clammy with perspiration.

'I'll just loosen your shirt, Mr Robinson,' she said, rapidly undoing his shirt buttons to enable the meagre chest to move more freely.

The patient's anxious eyes stared up at her and his breathing became more laboured as he looked at the strange nurse.

Jenna glanced at the table beside his armchair.

'Does he have a Ventolin inhaler?' she asked Mrs Robinson. The urgency of her tone made Mr Robinson more anxious, so that his breathing became even more laboured.

'I was getting the prescription today.' Mrs Robinson's voice was defensive. 'It takes forty-eight hours to get one from the surgery, and I forgot to place it earlier.' Her face had become harassed.

'I've brought it with me.' Daniel's calm voice swung all their heads in his direction, and Jenna saw the displeased expression on his face as he looked at her. She also saw the astonishment on Muriel's, and suddenly realised what she, Jenna, had done. She had taken over Muriel's patient. Jenna knew she could explain why her response to Harry Robinson's distress had been so prompt when they eventually left the flat, but at the moment she could say nothing.

'I think you can let Nurse Thomas take over now,' Daniel said drily, his eyes cold.

Jenna stepped aside. There was no apology in her expression, and this annoyed him further. One of those bold, unfeeling nurses, he thought, putting his bag down on the table beside Mr Robinson and taking the patient's pulse.

He was quite wrong in his supposition. Jenna was suffering from shock—shock at her precipitate behaviour. She knew, better than most, not to agitate an asthmatic.

Mr Robinson's breathing, by now, was so tight he was unable to speak. His face was paler and damper and his lips were blue.

'I'm going to give you an injection,' Daniel told him, smiling down at him. 'You've had it before.' The doctor's calm voice and familiarity of person soothed the distressed man so that the anxious expression in the blue eyes subsided a little.

Daniel did not bother to wash his hands; the patient needed the injection now. Muriel already had the paper off a ten-millimetre syringe and the needle attached. Daniel handed her the aminophylline and she gave him the syringe. She sawed off the top of the ampoule and he drew up the fluid after rechecking the dose.

Mr Robinson winced as the needle went into the vein. Slowly Daniel pushed the plunger and removed the needle when the fluid was given.

The two nurses, the doctor and Mrs Robinson stood without moving. Only the dog's whine from the bedroom disturbed the silence.

Gradually Mr Robinson's breathing improved and his face lost its pinchiness. The damp grey-brown streaks of his hair lay across his forehead like strands of sea grass left by the tide. He tried to raise his hand, but it fell back, his exhaustion almost complete.

Daniel drew the shirt across his chest as gently as a

mother would have done. Jenna's love, which she thought had been imagined, flowered once more, so that she wished she had been that shirt beneath his hand, and she burned with the force of her emotion. It disconcerted her to such an extent that she did not hear Daniel say to Muriel, 'Can you stay for a while?' or hear her assent.

It was Mrs Robinson's moving across Jenna's line of vision that drew her back to where she was.

'I'll make a cup of tea,' Mrs Robinson said.

Daniel stretched out a hand to delay her. 'Before you do, Mrs Robinson, I think we should admit your husband to hospital.'

Mrs Robinson's shoulders sagged with relief. 'If you think so, Dr Daniel,' she said.

He smiled down at the worn face. 'I do.' His voice was firm.

Mr Robinson did not speak, but his wife's relief was reflected in his eyes.

Daniel stayed a little longer to make sure the patient's improvement continued. 'I'll phone for an ambulance.' He glanced about the room. 'I wish you'd have a home help,' he said, smiling kindly at Mrs Robinson.

'My son won't hear of it,' she said. 'Says we can't afford it, not with him redundant and the children to provide for.' A look of despair crept into the tired eyes. 'I try to keep the place clean, but the kids. . .' She shrugged.

Daniel sighed. It was a sigh of defeat. 'Perhaps if I had a word with him,' he said, knowing the reply, but needing to try.

'Oh, no!' Mrs Robinson became agitated. 'He'd be furious! It's his pride, you see.'

The lines on Daniel's face deepened fractionally. He glanced up and met the eyes of the dark-haired nurse and recognised the compassion he saw in their depth. Perhaps he had been too hasty in his judgement, perhaps

she was not as unfeeling as he had supposed, and yet—
hadn't her handling of Mr Robinson shown a lack of
sensitivity?

The smile he was going to give her never reached his
lips, and Jenna felt his coldness. It seemed more than
her precipitate behaviour warranted, and it disconcerted
her afresh.

Then her optimistic nature rescued her once more.
Never mind, she said to herself, I'll change all that.
Didn't she have the attributes to do so? Wasn't she an
excellent nurse? Charming, attractive, sexy. A smile lit
her eyes as she enumerated her qualities, and it reached
her lips, irradiating her face. She was laughing at herself,
for she knew she had qualities on the debit side. She
was volatile and quick to anger.

Daniel's expression became more grim. He had interpreted her smile as an attempt to attract him and was
disgusted. A sick man lay within touching distance of
this woman, and she was looking at the doctor in
attendance like that. She was not a nurse. Her looks and
figure, her provocativeness, belonged to a much older
profession.

The depth of his feeling astonished him. No woman
had ever affected him like this before, and he could not
understand why he was so angry. It made him resent
the dark, sultry woman all the more.

He drew a sheet of notepaper and a brown envelope
from his bag, and, sitting at the table, concentrated his
thoughts on writing the letter to the casualty officer on
duty at Swansford General, and put the new nurse out
of his mind.

After a quiet word with Mr Robinson and a nod to
Muriel, he went towards the door. Jenna, who had not
heard him ask Muriel to stay, too busy with her own
musings, thought they were leaving as well, and followed him.

Daniel was about to grasp the door-handle when he

felt her behind him. He swung round so sharply that his bag almost hit her. They were so close he could see the smoothness of her skin, its Italian colouring, and felt a sudden urge to touch it. This angered him so much that his fair skin reddened, and he glanced across at Muriel as if for help. She only saw his anger.

'We're not leaving yet, Jenna,' she said quickly.

Jenna reached for the door-handle and opened the door without a word, hiding her disconcertion behind a bland expression.

The thought that she had followed him to perform this little courtesy made Daniel even more furious—furious because he had misread her motive and he was angry with himself, but he glared at her, barely able to bring himself to say, 'Thank you,' so that the words shot out abruptly.

Jenna, who could usually read men very well, was so occupied with her own embarrassment that she failed to see beyond his anger to the emotional disturbance her closeness had caused him. Even though she had managed to turn her mistake to her own advantage and so appear not too much of a fool, she felt no triumph, just a sudden misery. He was formidable in his fury. His anger should have dampened her feelings for him, but it didn't. It roused them even more, for his anger held passion, a passion she could relate to.

After he had gone, she said to Muriel, 'Would you like me to wait here for the ambulance while you carry on with the work?'

Muriel glanced at Mr Robinson, whose eyes were closed.

'Er—no.' Then, realising that her words sounded as if she lacked confidence in Jenna and knowing how important it was not to give this impression to the Robinsons, especially as Jenna was to be their nurse, Muriel said, 'We'll both wait. I need to speak to the ambulance men anyway,' and she smiled.

Jenna guessed why Muriel had spoken so and was saddened, but hoped she would be able to change the older nurse's opinion. Perhaps when she explained. . .

When the ambulance came Jenna hung back so that Muriel could speak to Mr Robinson. He had become agitated when she had approached him, and she hid her distress by turning away to collect Muriel's bag.

'I'll join you in the car,' said Muriel, sensing Jenna's discomfort and handing her the keys. 'Take the bag with you.'

Muriel joined her soon afterwards. They caught up with the ambulance at the junction, but turned left in the opposite direction. Muriel did not speak until they arrived at their next case. Then she switched off the engine and turned to face Jenna.

'I'd like to explain,' Jenna said before Muriel could speak. 'My reaction to Mr Robinson's distress was a reflex. You see, my mother is an asthmatic and I've had to help her on quite a few occasions, so I just automatically. . .' She did not finish the sentence.

Muriel placed her hand on Jenna's arm. 'I'm sorry.' She smiled gently. 'How is she now?'

The sadness which had darkened Jenna's features lifted as she said, 'My father took her to Arizona and the climate's suiting her. She's very much better there.'

'That's wonderful!' Muriel's face radiated her pleasure. 'We'll just have to explain that to Dr Daniel and the Robinsons.'

'I'd rather you didn't tell Dr White,' said Jenna, thinking he might take the explanation as an excuse.

Muriel gave her a doubtful look. 'Well, if you're sure—but he'd understand. He's a very caring person.'

'Yes, I can see that,' Jenna said, thinking silently, where the patients are concerned, but not where I come into his life, as she remembered his anger. 'But he may think the explanation wasn't enough. I did make Mr

Robinson's condition worse by approaching him as a stranger.'

Muriel had to admit the truth of what Jenna was saying. 'Well, I'm sure it will come right.' She tried to sound reassuring, but she knew how intense Daniel could be, so an underlying doubt coloured her words.

I've not made a very good start, thought Jenna as they left the car.

CHAPTER TWO

IT WAS after eleven o'clock when they returned to the Health Centre. Jenna had helped wash, dress and lift, using a hoist, Mrs Alice Hayes, a patient suffering from muscular dystrophy. They had left the lady in her electric wheelchair, which she manipulated using two fingers, the only movement she was able to make.

The home help arrived as the two nurses were leaving.

'I look forward to seeing you again, Nurse,' Mrs Hayes said, courage shining from her eyes.

'Alice makes up for the grumbles you encounter from some of the other patients,' said Muriel. 'I don't know how she stays so cheerful, especially as she lives on her own.'

Jenna showed her surprise. 'She hasn't a family?'

'A daughter who has four children and a lorry-driver husband who's away on trips quite a bit.'

Muriel turned into the Health Centre car park. 'She's well covered by the services on offer. The nurses go in three times a day. We also have an evening and night service which provides the rest. A home help comes in the morning and at tea-time to give Alice her meals.'

Jenna was impressed, and said so.

They hurried through the doors into the reception area. 'We'll just have a quick cup of coffee and see if we have any messages, then fly out again,' Muriel decided.

They hurried along the corridor. 'You can catch the doctors now,' Muriel explained, 'and get any prescriptions for dressing, et cetera, from them then.'

Muriel opened a door marked Staff, and Jenna found herself in a room overlooking the back of the Health

Centre. Flowers in tubs brightened a grey and pink patio which she could see through the french windows.

'We sit out there sometimes,' Muriel told her.

They were the first to arrive. Muriel handed a mug of black coffee to Jenna, wrinkling her nose in distaste. 'Ugh! I don't know how you can drink it like that,' she said.

The door opened. 'Pour one for me, will you, Muriel?'

The voice was so like Daniel's that Jenna expected to see him, and her pulse bounded, but it was a man who had a look of Daniel, but one who lacked his presence.

'Let me introduce you to the nurse who's taking over from me first,' Muriel said. Her face was not as welcoming as it had been for Daniel. 'Jenna Reid.' She turned to Jenna, who was a little behind her. 'This is Daniel's brother, Richard White.' She was between them so they could not shake hands. 'I'll just get some more milk.' She left the room.

As the door closed behind her, Richard said, 'Hel-lo!' The blue eyes were darker than his brother's and were lit with appreciation as they looked Jenna over. It was a look she was familiar with, compounded of desire and relish. This man she could deal with, and after Daniel's coldness it was a relief. She smiled, not realising how inviting her smile appeared to Richard until he came close to her and put his arm round her waist.

She was still holding her mug of coffee, and it slurped as she pushed him away. 'Now, now, mustn't touch,' she said firmly, smiling to take the sting from her words. After all, she would have to work with him, and she did not want to alienate him just yet.

His arm went round her again just as Daniel came into the room and saw what to him seemed an intimate picture. He had not heard her rebuff; he just saw her smiling up into his brother's face.

This nurse would have to go. None of the men at the Health Centre would be safe otherwise. First it had been himself and now it was his brother. He would not acknowledge a sudden flash of jealousy—it was too ridiculous.

'Richard!' Daniel's voice barked like a command, and his brother jumped back, his sudden movement upsetting Jenna's coffee.

'Oh, Daniel,' he said, his hand on his heart, 'don't do that. You might give me a heart attack!'

Jenna detected guilt behind the jesting protestation as she brushed the spilt coffee from her uniform. She found out why when Daniel said,

'Your wife was on the phone just now. She said she couldn't get an answer from yours.'

'She should have tried here.' Richard's tone was impatient. 'Do you know what she wanted?'

Daniel's expression was grim. Did he ever smile? wondered Jenna.

'She wants you to collect Amanda from school.'

Richard's face, which was ugly with irritation, softened as he said, 'Of course I will.'

'Well, you'd better ring her then, and tell her so.' Daniel's tone had lost its hardness, but his expression as he looked at Jenna was still grim, and she supposed it was because he had found her with his brother's arm about her, and blamed her.

The injustice of this roused her volatile spirit, and she glared at Daniel from beneath hooded lids. He was so irate at her supposed seduction of his brother that he did not see her anger, just how her sudden flush increased the attractiveness of her face, making it duskily alluring. He resented her all the more because it aroused him, and, if it aroused him, his brother would surely be unable to withstand it. Daniel knew Richard would not even try. It was up to him, Daniel, to protect his susceptible brother and so spare Susan, his sister-in-law, further pain.

Muriel's return with a carton of milk broke the tension between the three of them.

'Coffee?' She glanced at the two men. Trouble, she thought, seeing Daniel's angry face and observing Richard's stiff expression. Jenna? What a catalyst this girl's going to be, she mused.

'Thanks,' said Daniel, dropping a pile of case-notes with his visiting book on to the coffee-table. It was large enough to accommodate half a dozen easy-chairs around it. Jenna was standing by the table which held the coffee. Mugs with different logos stood beside the percolater. Muriel poured the coffee and handed Daniel's to him. Amusement crept into Jenna's eyes as she noted the saying on Daniel's which read, 'You don't have to be mad to work here, but it helps,' and wondered how long it would be before this man drove her mad with aggravation.

Daniel looked up, and seeing the laughter in her eyes, thought at first it was directed at himself, but then he saw it was his mug she was looking at and an involuntary smile, which he would have snatched back if he could, crossed his face, chasing the lines accumulated by years in general practice—anger, despair, happiness, relief— from his face, relaxing it so that he looked even more handsome, and she fell in love with him all over again.

'Sorry I'm late.' Penny's voice came from the door, much to Daniel's relief.

He smiled at her more attractively than he would have done normally as a result, and hope rose in the fair girl's heart.

'We've left you some coffee. Would you like me to pour it for you?'

Penny's amazement was reflected on Muriel's face and she almost wished she was not retiring. She had never known so many surprises in a morning before.

'Er—thank you,' Penny accepted, blushing.

Unreasonably, as Daniel handed Penny her mug, he

blamed Jenna again, for his leading Penny to suppose he was interested in her. He knew the girl was infatuated with him and he had been meticulous in behaviour towards her, as he was to any of the females who were attracted to him. He was practised in deflecting their attentions.

'No hitches in Mr Robinson's transfer to hospital?' he asked Muriel.

'No. I managed to dissuade his wife from going with him. She was exhausted, and the grandchildren will be home at three-thirty.'

'Good. Anything else?'

Muriel mentioned some prescriptions and Daniel wrote them. Jenna and Muriel left Penny discussing one of the patients with Richard. She was his nurse, while Jenna would be Daniel's.

The rest of the morning passed quickly. Mrs Dickens greeted them with, 'It was my bath day yesterday. I had the immersion on and my clean clothes out all ready.' The lines on the round face were cut deeply, but Jenna realised the patient's crossness was due more to the pain of her arthritis than to her displeasure.

'I'm very sorry,' said Muriel quietly. 'It won't happen again.'

Jenna was surprised that Muriel had not told Mrs Dickens that she had phoned her daughter about the change in the bath day, and resolved to ask her why when they had left the house.

The bath took some time, as Mrs Dickens's movements were limited. Jenna noted the bath aids and made a mental note to ask Muriel where the centre to procure such things was.

As they drove to the next patient Jenna asked Muriel why she had not mentioned phoning Mrs Dickens's daughter.

Muriel negotiated a sharp corner before replying.

'You never know when a child on a skateboard will

shoot out,' she explained, then continued, 'I didn't tell
Mrs Dickens because it would have caused friction
between mother and daughter, and there's enough of
that already. It's difficult to live in the house with a
disabled person, especially when they complain a lot, as
Dorothy Dickens does. Mind you, she had a lot to
complain about.' Muriel stopped the car outside St
Stephen's old people's home, on the estate. 'It's super
inside,' she said. 'Nice self-contained flats with a
warden. I think I'll put my name down now,' she joked.

At the end of the morning Muriel dropped Jenna at
the Health Centre. 'See you at two o'clock,' she said. 'I
must go home and let the dog out.'

Jenna wondered if one of the cars in the car park
belonged to Daniel, and hoped it didn't. She was not
eager to see him again just yet. She needed time to sort
out her emotions.

Penny turned bulging cheeks towards her as she came
into the staff lounge, both hands clutching a large roll.
After swallowing the last bit, she drank some milk, then
said, 'How did your morning go?' She seemed excited.

Jenna gave a big sigh and sank into one of the
armchairs. 'Don't ask!' she groaned.

Penny pushed a packet of sandwiches and a carton of
milk towards her.

'I seem to do everything wrong, and Dr White. . .'
Jenna pulled a face. 'He definitely does *not* like me!'

'But he seems to like me,' said Penny, still glowing
from Daniel's attention.

A twinge of jealousy caught Jenna unwares. She had
never experienced the emotion before. Just something
else for her to adjust to, she thought as she forced a
smile on to her face.

Penny frowned. 'You do think so, don't you?' taking
Jenna's silence for doubt.

'Er——' Jenna dragged her mind away from herself
'—yes, I expect so.'

'You don't sound too sure.' Penny's glow was rapidly subsiding.

Jenna frowned. 'I don't know him. How can I tell?'

'Oh, come on, Jenna! With all your experience. . .'

This was too much, on top of the aggravations of the morning. 'What experience?' Jenna demanded crossly. 'Experience of fielding unwelcome attentions, yes, but as an authority on love—no.'

Penny's mouth gaped. She knew her friend was volatile, but she had not expected her words to produce such a vehement response.

'Sorry,' she apologised. 'It's just that I think I'm in love with him,' and her eyes became dreamy.

You're not the only one, thought Jenna. I'm sure there must be others as well. Perhaps we could form a club—and the idea was so amusing that she laughed.

'It's not funny,' said Penny, pushing crumbs from her roll into a mound, a hurt expression on her face.

Jenna was immediately contrite. 'No, of course it isn't—I'm sorry. It's just that I've had a rotten morning,' and she told Penny about Mr Robinson.

'How awful!' Penny's face was full of sympathy. 'Would you like me to explain to Daniel?'

'No!' Jenna's voice was sharp.

Penny gave her a doubtful look. 'But he'll think——'

'I don't care what he thinks,' Jenna interrupted her, and at that moment she didn't. She bit into her sandwich savagely. 'Men!' she mumbled with her mouth full.

The rest of the day passed without further incident. The delay at the Robinsons' had put them back, so they were having to do dressings which should have been done in the morning. Their last visit was a removal of stitches from an appendicectomy wound.

'I thought you were coming this morning, Nurse,' Mrs Johns said as she led the way to her son's room. 'I was just going to get the messages.' Annoyance underlined her words.

Muriel was hot and tired. Climbing seven flights to this flat because the lift was out of order hadn't helped.

'An emergency this morning held us back,' she explained evenly.

Jenna admired the older nurse's self-control, feeling sure she would not have been able to discipline herself in such a manner, and wondering if she should give up the district there and then. She was not sure she had the qualities she saw in Muriel.

They entered a bedroom, the windows of which overlooked the countryside, as had the Robinsons'. The sun was still shining and the view was the same. It was almost as if time had stood still. Posters of pop groups decorated the wall, Madonna being most noticeable.

'I'll leave you to it,' said Mrs Johns, retreating quickly.

A twenty-year-old youth was lying on the bed. He looked up from a magazine. He was well made and good-looking. Throwing the magazine aside, he said, 'I want you to take my stitches out,' eyeing Jenna boldly.

Before Muriel could speak, Jenna said, 'Very well,' glancing at the older nurse for affirmation.

Muriel nodded. She had heard the steel beneath Jenna's quietly spoken words, and was curious to see how the young woman would handle the situation.

Muriel handed the stitch pack to Jenna, who opened it without touching its contents. She bent over Mark Johns. 'Loosen the top of your trousers,' she said with an expressionless face.

'With pleasure,' Mark complied with alacrity, his eyes gleaming. His jeans were down in a moment, exposing blue-striped Y-fronts. He was about to lower these when Jenna said sweetly, 'I'll do that.'

Mark's eyes widened.

Jenna turned down the top just sufficiently to expose the dressing.

'I bet you enjoy doing this.' Mark glanced at her in a suggestive way.

She deliberately misunderstood him and said, 'Yes, I quite like taking stitches out. I've done quite a few,' and pulled off the dressing, some of the micro-pore sticking to the hair now growing from the shaved area.

'Ouch!' he shrieked, moving away from her with an aggrieved expression on his face.

'Sorry,' Jenna said blithely. 'It does sometimes stick.' She moved towards the door. 'I'm just going to wash my hands.'

'First on the right,' he said, his tone suspicious.

She was back in a moment. Muriel was dropping a stitch cutter on to the opened dressing pack.

'What's that for?' Mark's eyes were apprehensive.

'To cut the stitch with,' explained Jenna, and proceeded to remove the first one.

When it did not hurt him Mark's expression once again became provocative. Glancing at him, she caught that look and removed the next stitch.

'Ow!' His expression changed to one of complaint.

'Sorry,' she said. 'I just can't concentrate when you look at me like that.' Her voice was heavy with sarcasm as she removed the next stitch, which also pulled a little.

'Please!' he begged, looking up at her pathetically.

'They do sometimes pull,' she repeated. 'I'm sure the rest of them will come out easily if you stop undressing me.'

His fair skin flushed.

Jenna removed the rest of the stitches quickly and painlessly.

'My mother will report you for this!' he snapped aggressively, his handsome face ugly.

'Really?' Jenna raised her eyebrows. 'For what?' Her dark eyes were contemptuous as she tied up the dirty dressing bag. 'Some stitches are embedded deeply,' she pointed to the two reddened areas where the stitches had pulled when removed, 'and do sting a little.' She held his eyes, her own dark ones black with disdain. 'The redness will subside now.'

'Still——'

'That will do, Mark.' Muriel's voice was firm.

But it was a disgruntled Mark they left lying on the bed. His pride had been hurt.

'I think you handled that young man extremely well.' Muriel glanced at her young colleague with admiration.

'I've had plenty of practice.' Jenna smiled. 'Sometimes the male patients don't see me as a nurse, they just see my face and figure.' There was no conceit in her tone, just resignation. 'It takes a little time, but they are converted eventually.'

Muriel laughed. 'I bet they are!' She was beginning to like this girl, and, as she thought this, she realised that she also had made a similar judgement even though unconsciously. Then her face became serious.

'You might have some trouble from that family. It's happened before.'

'I'll face that when it comes,' said Jenna, feeling her heart sink. It was to come sooner than she expected.

Penny was waiting for her when the two nurses arrived back. 'Dr Daniel wants to see you, Jenna.' She looked apprehensive.

Jenna frowned. 'Do you know why?' she asked. She had never had such a dreadful day.

'No, but he didn't sound pleased.' Penny's face was still apprehensive. 'He's writing up his case-notes in his surgery. You can't miss it—his name's on the door.'

'Would you like me to come with you?' offered Muriel, sensing Jenna's disquiet behind the calm face.

'No, thanks.' Jenna brushed a strand of dark hair into place, and straightened her dress. Taking a deep breath, she said, 'Right,' and left them.

Outside the door marked 'Dr Daniel White' in bold black letters, she paused again, then knocked.

'Come in.'

Daniel was sitting behind a teak desk. The window was to the right of it. Light-painted walls blended with the green carpet and curtains to give an overall calm effect to the room. An examination couch of a standard variety stood along the wall to the left. A teak bookcase was filled with medical books, their well-used covers the only worn note in the otherwise spotless room. Jenna found them comforting. They looked like old friends.

Daniel's desk was untidy, with a pile of case-notes on one side perilously near the edge. The back of a picture frame faced Jenna, and she wondered who it was. She knew he wasn't married.

The thoughts and impressions were fleeting. The man behind the desk was looking at her with cold blue eyes. The angles of his face were tense and sharp. It had a honed appearance. It was an introspective face, a suppressed face, and Jenna wondered just what it was he was suppressing.

In spite of her apprehension she could not help but be caught by the quality of the man. He was more than handsome; he had a refinement, an integrity, an uprightness, and her heart was lost once more, so that she stood silent before him, unaware of how proudly she held her head or of how her foreignness set her apart. It was as if an Italian woman of seductive beauty was standing there, and when he did not speak for a moment, caught as she had been, but in a different way, Jenna could stand the build-up of tension no longer and said,

'You wanted to see me, Dr White?'

Daniel was disconcerted. He had expected to hear an Italian accent instead of the pure English she spoke. To give himself time to recover himself, he put the cap on to his pen and threw it on the desk.

'Yes, Miss Reid.' The ordinariness of her surname seemed out of place when applied to this woman. She should have had a surname like. . . These riotous

thoughts were so out of character that he was appalled
at himself. It was almost as if he was besotted with this
woman. His face hardened as he fought against her
magnetism.

A darkness came over Jenna's features as she saw his
stiffening, but this sombreness attracted Daniel even
more, so that his fist came down hard on the desk as he
shot to his feet, in his annoyance with himself. The pain
in his hand seemed to restore his perspective.

Jenna had not moved. She had seen violent men
before.

'Miss Reid,' Daniel had control of himself now, 'Mrs
Johns had just phoned with a complaint directed at you.'
He paced up and down behind the desk, his hands
behind his back, his head bent. Stopping suddenly, he
looked at her from under lowering brows. Her stillness
and lack of expression disconcerted him. He was used
to people reacting differently to his anger—tears, defiance—and he would have thought this woman would
have been sure to respond in a similar way, but her lack
of reaction he put down to dumb insolence.

'Haven't you anything to say?' he barked, and the
release of his anger at himself by directing it at her
suddenly made him ashamed. 'What——' He was going
to say, 'is your excuse?' in a less abrasive manner, but
she interrupted him, and this fuelled his anger afresh.

'How can I answer when I don't know what you're
charging me with?'

It was spoken calmly, in a quiet tone, with her head
up.

The justness of her words embarrassed him. She had
so overwhelmed his senses that he had not realised that
he had not told her of what she was accused.

'Mrs Johns said that you deliberately hurt her son by
pulling out his stitches roughly.'

Jenna had had many complaints directed against her

by rebuffed males, but this was a new one. It attacked her professionally, and she was not going to ignore that.

Her body stiffened, her dark eyes becoming fierce. She was magnificent in her anger. There flashed before Daniel's eyes a picture of her dressed as in Roman times, white folds across her chest, draped seductively about her, her hair high on her head with curls down her back.

Am I going mad? a voice screamed inside him. His face flushed, and he glanced at the photograph on his desk, reaching to touch its silver frame. The woman who looked out at him with an expression as cool as the silver had a patrician beauty—oval face, fair skin, auburn hair, cool blue eyes. It comforted him.

Jenna, seeing his flush, thought it was due to his anger, but did not let it dismay her.

'She didn't tell you, I suppose, that her son's stitches had bitten deeply into his flesh and that anyone removing them would have caused some discomfort?' Her face was expressionless, but as she added, 'Nor did she tell you that I had to rebuff her son's obnoxious advances, I take it?' Her face flushed.

Daniel could not help himself. He had to ask, 'Are you sure you didn't encourage them?' He had to know. The thought that she might have encouraged the boy hurt him too much, and this sudden knowledge shocked him to such an extent that he sat down abruptly, and the blue eyes staring at him from the photograph seemed to be accusing him, which did not help.

The silence in the room was complete. The double glazing prevented any outside noise from being heard in the room.

Jenna was appalled. Her attraction for Daniel was unchanged, but that he should think   ask such a question, gripped her with such force that it rocked her, and, indeed, she did sway a little.

Daniel wanted to leap to his feet, beg her forgiveness, but he was unable to bring himself to do so. Shock at the depth of his feelings lay upon him like a great weight, holding him in the chair.

Jenna wanted to scream, How dare you? but was held like Daniel, speechless with anger.

Then a child's voice calling, 'Daddy, Daddy!' outside broke the emotional tension that bound her.

'I'm tempted not to reply to that question, Dr White.' She was surprised at how calm she sounded—she was seething inside. 'I would have thought that a man in your profession would have had more insight, but I can't let it pass. I did not encourage him.' The evenness of her tone was more impressive than a tirade. 'I can't help being built the way I am, any more than you can help being handsome, and no doubt attractive to women, but I do not. . .' here she paused for emphasis '. . . deliberately lure men.' The sarcasm in her voice hit him like a slap in the face.

Jenna was right. Hadn't he moaned when he thought she was trying to attract him? Daniel was caught by his own conceit, but it restored his sanity. He had been unjust. He should not have condemned Jenna like that. The attraction for her was still there, but he could control it now.

'You're quite right,' he said. 'The ordinary people in this world envy the good-looker, but little do they know what a price we have to pay sometimes.' His face was serious, his fantasies quenched. The nurse opposite him was just that—a nurse—not a Roman goddess. Daniel took a deep breath. 'If you have any more trouble with the male patients come and tell me.' His eyes were gentle, and this was worse than his anger.

His softening made Jenna want to melt into his arms, cry out the misery the day had brought her on his shoulder. Instead, she just said, 'Thank you.' But her face remained sombre.

Suddenly Daniel wanted to see her smile. He said, rising to his feet, 'I'll do the same with you. I'll tell you if I have trouble with women falling at my feet.' He laughed.

Jenna smiled. 'It's a bargain.'

Daniel opened the door for her. She felt relaxed enough to smile up into the face that made her heart stop and say, 'I hope we'll be able to work well together.'

Her words reminded him of her behaviour at the Robinsons', and it was his face that became sombre now.

'Yes. I hope so too.'

Jenna saw the doubt in his eyes and knew the reason for it, but could not bring herself to explain.

'Daniel!'

A woman of grace and elegance was walking down the corridor towards them, a shopping bag in her hand. Her auburn hair was swept into a french pleat, her oval face was perfect in its symmetry, the fair skin unblemished, and her figure was slim, like a model's. She was wearing a pale blue suit that matched her eyes, and it was these eyes that spoilt her perfection; they were brittle and lacked warmth. She was almost the same height as the doctor and nearer his age, being about thirty-one.

Jenna had always thought of herself as tall at five foot seven, but she had to look up at this woman, who was resting her hand on Daniel's arm in a proprietorial way.

'I thought you might give me a lift home,' the woman said. The blue eyes had softened.

Daniel's face brightened with pleasure. 'Elaine!' There was no mistaking the delight in his voice as he tucked her hand through his arm. It was more than delight, it was relief. He felt as if Elaine had rescued him, but from what he would not admit to himself.

Who was this woman? wondered Jenna, and her heart contracted with distress.

'Elaine, let me introduce you to our new District Nursing Sister, Jenna Reid, Muriel's replacement. This is Elaine Winton, my wife. . .' Jenna's heart felt as if it had stopped '. . . to be.'

'Darling!' Elaine's adoring glance left Daniel's face as she held out her hand to Jenna.

Jenna's heart was bounding again. She took the slim hand extended towards her and felt its coldness as she held it in her warm one.

To others less sensitive than Jenna, Elaine appeared delighted to meet her, but Jenna suspected the cool beauty, the calculating eyes.

It was obvious that Daniel was besotted with Elaine. He held her arm close to his side so that their bodies were touching.

'I was shopping in Swansford and I knew you'd give me a lift home.' Elaine's voice was as soft as the look Daniel was giving her.

They turned away, and Jenna might not have been there. Pain such as Jenna had never known caught her and she gasped, but the couple were too far away to hear.

How can this be? thought Jenna, staring at the backs of the tall doctor and his lady. The fair and auburn heads joined for a moment as he bent to hear what Elaine was saying. How can I be in love with this man? her heart wailed. But she was. She had never felt like this before, happy yet sad at the same time.

'There you are!' Penny touched her arm. 'Muriel's gone—said to tell you she'd see you tomorrow.' Then, seeing the sadness on her friend's face, she said, alarm making her voice sharp, 'What did Daniel say to you?'

Jenna took a deep breath. 'Actually, he was very nice.' She gave a low laugh. 'After I'd straightened him out over a thing or two.'

Penny laughed. 'I thought I saw someone with him,' she said, peering ahead.

They had reached the reception area. Daniel, with Elaine, could be seen crossing the car park.

'Yes. It was his fiancée,' Jenna said. 'You didn't tell me he was engaged.'

Penny was so shocked that she did not hear the accusation in Jenna's voice. 'Engaged?' Her face had paled. 'I didn't know!' It was almost a wail.

Jenna caught hold of her friend's arm and pulled her out of the Health Centre. Penny looked stunned. 'Give me the keys,' Jenna demanded in a firm voice.

Penny pulled them from her pocket, but they fell to the ground. Jenna was upset to see tears in her friend's eyes. Retrieving the keys, she pushed Penny into the Mini.

Jenna had stayed with Penny in Swansford before she accepted this post, so she knew her way to the flat. It was in a good part of the town, overlooking the river, where swans gracefully raised their heads. They had given their name to the town.

The flats were two years old. Penny's was on the top floor of the three-storeyed block. Jenna parked the Mini in the space provided at the back of the block.

Penny just sat, her head bent. 'Come on, Penny,' Jenna's voice was all soothing encouragement, 'let's get you a cup of tea and talk it out.'

Penny allowed Jenna to lead her. When they were in the flat, Jenna put on the kettle in the small kitchen, which was bright with geraniums on the windowsill.

'I didn't know he was engaged!' wailed Penny.

'Was it a secret?' Jenna reached for the teapot. It was shaped like a cat and she had laughed when she had first seen it, but it did not make her laugh now. She knew how Penny was feeling. Wasn't she feeling the same—miserable?

'Well, it was common knowledge that he was seeing someone.' Penny took the mug of tea from Jenna. 'But no one had seen him with her, so. . .' Penny shrugged. 'They must have become engaged just recently, or we all would have known.'

The girls took their tea into the lounge, which overlooked the river. A walkway ran along its side, with seats placed at intervals for the public.

'Had Daniel ever given you reason to suppose he was fond of you?' asked Jenna as they sat down. 'And what about Charlie?'

'Oh, Charlie.' Penny dismissed her childhood sweetheart with a wave of her hand. 'And Daniel did,' she said, with a sob. 'You saw how attentive he was today.'

'That's not quite what I meant,' said Jenna gently. She had a sudden sympathy for Daniel. She knew only too well how a simple gesture could be misinterpreted by someone who was infatuated, but at the same time she was annoyed with Daniel. He must have known how Penny felt about him, for her friend was not sophisticated enough to hide her feelings. I only hope I am, Jenna mused.

'But I thought you loved Charlie,' she persisted.

'Oh, it's all right for you.' Bitterness made Penny's voice sharp. 'You've only got to snap your fingers and the men fall at your feet. You've never fallen in love, so you don't know!' It came out in a wail.

Penny's words hurt, and Jenna could think of nothing to say in reply.

Penny's hand flew to her mouth when she realised what she had said. 'Oh, Jen,' she groaned, 'forgive me!' She wasn't hypocrite enough to add that she didn't mean it because, in a way, she had.

'That's all right.' Jenna went over to her, her colour sense cringing at the brightly coloured orange Dralon of the armchair Penny was sitting in, and patted her friend's shoulder.

The whole flat was a reflection of Penny's cheerfulness. Each room was bright. The bedrooms were yellow and green with décor in varying tones to match.

Jenna sank into the armchair beside her, too exhausted to stand a moment longer. A sudden yearning for her parents swept over her, but they were in Arizona. She had no one in this country, and for the first time she wished she weren't an only child. Her mother's health had been poor and the Reids had decided not to have children; it was just chance that her mother became pregnant when she was thirty-nine. Their delight in Jenna had enfolded her with love, and it was this Jenna missed. They had preferred their own company and were wrapped up in each other and the child.

Jenna had been brought up in Surrey, but her training in London, followed by midwifery and district, had caused her to lose touch with the friends of her childhood. She hoped this infatuation with Daniel had not turned Penny against her, for she valued Penny's friendship too much.

She drank her tea. 'I'll make some spaghetti bolognaise,' she said, rising to collect the empty mugs.

'Not that delicious spaghetti bolognaise you made in training?' Penny's eyelids were still red and her face blotched, but her eyes had brightened.

'Yes,' called Jenna from the kitchen. She smiled to herself. Penny's infatuation with Daniel could not be too acute, or her interest in food would have waned. If Charlie would only come! Jenna thought.

As Jenna made the meal, she decided to put Daniel out of her mind. It's probably just my age, twenty-six and never been in love, so I think I've fallen for the first man who's really attracted me, she thought.

She sieved the spaghetti and divided it on to two plates. Her movements were vicious and some of it slipped on to the floor.

Who am I fooling? she thought. She threw the sauce on to the spaghetti and it splashed on to the worktops. She mopped up the mess, picked up the plates and went into the lounge. The doorbell rang as she handed Penny's plate to her.

'I'll go,' offered Jenna.

Penny sprang to her feet. 'That'll be Charlie!' She had rushed from the room before Jenna could move, and returned a minute later with a well-built young man, six feet tall, broad-shouldered, with an attractive face. His red hair was short and curly.

'It's good to see Charlie, isn't it, Jenna?' said Penny a little too brightly as she pulled him into the lounge.

'It certainly is.' Jenna's tone held a sarcastic note. 'Hi, Charlie!'

'Hi!' Charlie's eyes were for Penny; he didn't even bother to look at Jenna.

'Have you eaten?' asked Penny.

'Yes, thanks, but I wouldn't mind a nibble of you,' he said, putting his arms round her.

'I'll leave you two together,' Jenna said, taking her plate with her.

Penny didn't protest.

Jenna picked at her meal in the green bedroom, wishing the colours were not so deep. The irritations and emotional upsets of the day had left her too tense to eat more than a few mouthfuls.

I'll have to find a place of my own, she decided as she put the plate down on the green dressing-table, the remains of the spaghetti bolognaise clashing violently with it.

I wonder if I've made a mistake in coming to Swansford? she thought. Her last post was beginning to look more attractive, in spite of the sexual harassment she had had to contend with.

CHAPTER THREE

JENNA was reassured during the next two days. Muriel's hand-over was thorough and comprehensive, so that by the time Friday came Jenna was looking forward to assuming Muriel's responsibilities.

She had no further problems with the patients, the majority of whom were elderly. Her quiet unassuming manner reassured them.

Daniel was polite, though distant, but this did not bother her. In fact, she preferred it this way. The less she saw of him the less her heart was affected.

On Friday, after lunch, Muriel handed her a piece of paper with a name and address. 'I think it would be a good idea if you admit Mrs Green, as she's going to be your patient from now on,' she said. Her eyes were wistful. 'Daniel saw the lady at his surgery yesterday. She's seventy-eight and knocked her leg on the bus when it pulled up sharply. She has a nasty wound that he says is infected, and he thinks a nurse should visit her. If there isn't any improvement we're to let him know.'

Jenna had brought her own car, so it wasn't long before she was ringing the bell of a bungalow almost identical to Mrs Ledson's. Emma Green, bright-eyed and sprightly, answered it. She had a motherly figure and grey wavy hair, and Jenna liked her immediately.

The house was well furnished and spotless. Mrs Green showed Jenna into the lounge. Comfortable chairs, a gas fire and a cat completed the cosy picture of an elderly lady sitting beside a fire with her cat in the winter seen on so many cards.

'Shoo, Blackie!' She wafted her hand and the cat

ambled slowly from the room. 'He's as old as I am,' she said with a laugh.

Jenna put her bag down on one of the ladder-backed chairs after asking permission to do so.

'Are you going to do my dressing now?' Mrs Green's eyes were apprehensive.

'No,' Jenna smiled. 'I just came to introduce myself and to take a few details.'

Emma Green relaxed. 'Fire away,' she said.

Jenna sat in the other armchair and proceeded to note down Emma's family history and background. As she capped her pen when she had finished, Emma said,

'Would you like a cup of tea?'

Jenna now knew that Emma Green lived alone, that her husband had died five years ago, that her son was in Canada and her daughter in Australia. There was a niece in this country. She felt Emma's loneliness and said, 'I'd love a cup of tea. Can I make it for you?'

'Thank you.' Emma's eyes brightened. 'The kitchen's at the end of the hall. The teapot and caddy are out and the cups and saucers ready on the tray.' She smiled sheepishly. 'I put it ready in case.'

Jenna grinned, and pushed the footstool under Emma's leg.

The tea was soon made, and Jenna carried the tray with its delicate china back into the lounge.

When they were settled, Jenna said, 'You mentioned a niece. Does she visit you often?'

'She's staying with me at the moment.'

'Oh.' The word slipped from Jenna's lips before she could stop it. It sounded like an accusation.

'She had to go out,' explained Emma.

Jenna made no comment and led the conversation away from the niece by telling Emma when and how often her dressing would be done.

They had finished their tea and Jenna was taking the

tray. 'Just leave it in the kitchen,' said Emma, with a smile.

Jenna was in the hall when the bell rang.

'That'll probably be my niece, Nurse. Would you let her in, please?'

'Yes, Mrs Green.'

Jenna opened the door, balancing the tray in one hand. She nearly dropped it when she saw Daniel on the step.

'Muriel told me you were here,' he explained, eyeing the tray.

'Would you like a cup?' Jenna always found that attack was better than defence, and she had sensed his disapproval of the tea.

But she was mistaken. It was not disapproval of her wasting time taking tea with a patient that made him frown; it was alarm at the sudden leap his heart made when he saw her. He had managed to avoid direct contact with her since Wednesday and had thought the sensations she had roused then had just been because he was missing Elaine. But now. . .

'No, thank you.' He was still standing on the step, close enough for her to see a small healing scar where he had nicked himself shaving. 'Are you going to let me in?' He raised an impatient eyebrow.

'Er—yes.' Jenna was annoyed with herself for stammering like an adolescent schoolgirl. She stepped back hastily, and the tray tilted.

Daniel took it from her. Had he been right? Was Jenna attracted to him? The thought made his heart bound, alarming him further, and he decided afresh that Jenna Reid would have to go.

He walked without hesitation to the kitchen with Jenna following. She supposed his familiarity with the house was because he had been in so many similar ones.

When they entered the lounge, Emma Green's eyes

brightened with pleasure. 'I'm afraid Elaine's not here,' she said.

Jenna was dumbfounded. Elaine, Daniel's fiancée, was Emma Green's niece! Daniel's visit was not a professional one. He had come to see Elaine.

An irritated frown crossed Daniel's forehead.

'I thought she would be here when Sister arrived,' he said. 'She knew a visit was expected.' Then, realising he was criticising his fiancée in front of Jenna, he said, 'I suppose it must have been. . .'

'I told her to go,' said Emma. 'You know how restless she gets.'

Daniel did. It was one of the things. . .hastily he amended his thought. . .the only thing about Elaine he found difficult to accept.

'Anyway, I can manage perfectly well on my own,' Emma said defensively.

Daniel smiled, and Jenna sighed. If only he would smile at me like that, she mused.

Emma was not immune to Daniel's smile either. 'Elaine's a lucky girl,' she said, her sigh covering up Jenna's. I just hope she realises it, Emma thought. She had seen the warmth in the dark nurse's eyes as they had rested on Daniel for a moment.

The doorbell rang again. 'That must be Elaine this time,' said Emma.

This time she was right. Daniel let his fiancée in.

'I just popped to the shops,' she was saying as she preceded him into the lounge, a large bunch of flowers in her hand. 'I thought these might cheer you up after your fall,' she said, handing the bouquet of roses to her aunt.

Jenna tried to hear insincerity in her voice, but she couldn't. There was genuine warmth in the beautiful face smiling at Emma, who thanked her.

'Perhaps the nurse would put them in water for you,' Elaine added, turning to Jenna, her blue eyes cold.

'I think Sister Reid has more important things to do,' Emma told her. 'No doubt you'll be able to find a vase in the kitchen cupboard.' Her tone was dry.

Daniel had not spoken. He was watching Jenna's struggle to suppress her anger at being treated like a servant.

Feeling his eyes on her, she glanced in his direction and saw the amusement in them. Her anger slipped away and she smiled. There was an intimacy in the empathy between them that excluded Elaine, and it thrilled Jenna.

Elaine had not seen the swift interchange as she was accepting the flowers back from her aunt. 'I'll put them in water right away,' she said.

Guilt straightened Daniel's face. 'Let me help you,' he said, and out of the corner of his eye saw amusement in Jenna's. He felt like a married man who had been unfaithful to his wife, and it did not please him. All he wanted to do at that moment was to escape from this disturbing dark nurse.

He took the flowers from Elaine in one hand and hers with the other. At the lounge door he paused. He had remembered one of the reasons for his visit, and turned to face Jenna.

'I just want a word with Nurse,' he said, releasing Elaine's hand.

She took the flowers from him. 'I'll be in the kitchen,' she said with a smile.

Jenna had not moved. Her back was to the light, shadowing her face. It was dark, except for her eyes, which were intense. Daniel could see the suppressed passion burning behind them. For a moment he could not speak. His mouth was dry; perspiration broke out on his upper lip. 'Er. . .' he began.

Jenna could not prevent the smile. It was a smile that women of her powerful sexual attraction possessed. It held a promise, but there was more than a promise here; there was desire, and it rocked Daniel.

It was gone in a moment. He must have imagined it, he decided. This woman was bewitching him. Anger brought the saliva flowing into his mouth.

'We're having a party at my brother's house for Muriel's retirement,' he told her. 'She'd like you to come.'

He had made it obvious by his choice of words that he would be pleased if she did not accept. Devilment made Jenna answer, 'I'd love to—thank you.'

'Six-thirty, then.' His face was stiff. 'Penny knows where it is.' He turned away sharply.

Emma Green had watched the interchange with interest.

'You like Daniel, don't you?' she said as the door closed behind him.

'Yes and no,' Jenna said cautiously, for, although she had immediately taken to Emma, the elderly lady was Elaine's aunt. 'I really don't know him.'

'Elaine means to keep him,' Emma said quietly.

'Thanks for the warning,' Jenna said with a smile, keeping her tone light. 'I'll bear it in mind,' and she laughed as if Emma had made a joke. 'I'll be in tomorrow to change your dressing.'

'Thanks,' Emma smiled, but made no further comment.

When she made to rise Jenna pressed her back into the chair. 'I'll see myself out,' she told her.

As she passed through the hall and opened the front door she heard Daniel and Elaine laugh. A desolation such as she had never known swept over her, so that she had to clutch at the door-frame for support.

The kitchen door opened. Jenna straightened her back and stepped from the house before the couple could see her.

Muriel was still at the Health Centre when Jenna

returned. 'You didn't tell me Mrs Green was Dr White's fiancée's aunt,' Jenna said in as even a tone as she could.

Muriel's eyebrows rose. 'I didn't know Mrs Green was related to Elaine.' Her expression softened. 'So he finally asked her! I take it he caught you there to ask you to this do they're giving for me?'

'Yes.' Jenna did not realise how solemn she looked.

'Was there any trouble?' Muriel sensed an anguish in the other girl.

'No,' Jenna was quick to reply. 'Dr White came while I was there and his fiancée arrived a bit later.'

'Are you coming tonight?'

'Yes, of course,' Jenna smiled, but wished she had not accepted now.

Muriel handed her her bag. 'It's yours now,' she said.

Jenna could see Muriel was close to tears. 'It must be tough,' she remarked. Sympathy warmed her brown eyes.

'Yes, but I'll get over it.' Muriel smiled. 'Thirty years on the same district is like being a member of a large family. You see the children grow up and their children arrive. Marriages, divorces—you have to counsel them all. A district nurse's duties extend beyond those in hospital. There, the patients go home, but here they're in their own home.' She grinned. 'There I go, preaching again!' Then her face became serious. 'I just wanted to let you know what you're in for.'

'Thanks.' Jenna smiled. 'Are you going to sit back and put your feet up now?'

'No. I'm going to join the Women's Royal Voluntary Service. They'll keep me occupied,' said Muriel, rising to go. 'See you tonight.'

Jenna watched from the window as Muriel, straight-backed, crossed the car park to her car. In a way, she envied the retiring nurse, and wondered if she could absorb herself in her career as Muriel had done, but, even as she wondered, she knew it would not be enough.

That evening, in the multi-coloured green bedroom, Jenna surveyed her wardrobe. Her father had sold his chain of grocery stores to one of the big supermarkets when he had decided that his wife's health was more important than his business. The price he had received was more than generous, and he had provided Jenna with a monthly income which meant she could indulge in an occasional spending spree.

She had always loved clothes, and her tastes tended to be unusual. She bought Italian garments when she could, knowing how they suited her dark colouring.

The suit she took from the wardrobe was of green silk patterned with flowers. It made her look more exotic and it enfolded rather than clothed her. The skirt was just above her knees, its shortness drawing attention to the perfection of her legs. The top had elbow-length sleves, a V neckline and a peplum which emphasised her curvaceous hips.

Jenna, a creature of feeling, dressed to suit her mood. If she was miserable, she wore dark clothes; if happy, bright ones. What she did not realise was that no matter how subdued her garments were, when worn by her they became alive, vibrant. Even the plain gold chain she chose to complement her outfit glowed against her skin. Tonight she needed a morale-booster, so she slipped this dress on, knowing it would receive admiring glances.

She was brushing her curly hair, skilfully cut so that it curled about her face, when Penny called from outside her door,

'Ready?'

Jenna opened the door. 'Just my bag to collect,' she said, lifting a black suede bag from the bed.

'Wow!' Penny's eyes were round with envy. 'Why can't I look like that?'

'Would you believe it if I said the same about you?'

Jenna admired the fair freshness of her friend, whose simple blue dress was the colour of her eyes.

'You're just kidding—trying to make me feel good.' Penny's eyes were doubtful.

Jenna knew it would be useless to insist that she was being genuine, so she did not reply.

Richard White's house was in the old part of Swansford. It was set back from the road and overlooked the park. Cars were already in the drive, but Penny managed to find a space for her Mini.

As they stepped from the car, Penny glanced about her, her face brightening when she saw an almost identical Mini, also red, squeezed in between a Rover and a BMW.

'Charlie's here already,' she remarked. She did not want to lose Charlie, but Daniel still drew her, and her eyes became sad.

Jenna, seeing this, linked her arm in her friend's and said, 'Come on. At least we'll get a free feed!'

This brought a smile to Penny's face.

Before they could ring the bell, the door opened and a fair-haired woman holding a child's hand greeted them with, 'Amanda had me looking out for you. She wants to meet the new nurse.'

Penny laughed and turned to Jenna. 'Meet Richard's wife, Susan,' she said.

Jenna smiled as the tall woman with the serene face took her hand. There was a resignation in the smile that puzzled her.

'And this,' Penny knelt beside the fair child holding Susan's hand, 'is Amanda, who's a darling.'

Jenna was annoyed with Penny for not telling her that Amanda was blind. She recovered herself quickly and said, crouching beside the child so that she was level with her, 'Hello, Amanda.' A spontaneous love for all hurt and disabled people coloured her voice and glowed in her face. Daniel, stepping from the lounge at that moment, saw the change it wrought in her. Jenna's smile was relaxed and genuine. It held no wariness or reserve, and it attracted him even more. He saw not the alluring woman, only a sincere, enchanting one, and his breath caught in his throat.

Amanda put her arms round Jenna's neck and hugged her. 'I love you,' she said, sensing Jenna's sincerity.

Jenna laughed, and at the precise moment that she said, 'And I love you too,' her eyes met Daniel's, and the laughter in their depth changed to a sadness that tore at his heart and made his eyes bleak, but why, he would not admit to himself.

This bleakness Jenna interpreted as a coldness towards herself. She stood up and took Amanda's hand. Susan took the other one and they went forward. There was no sign of Daniel in the hall, and Jenna began to wonder if she had really seen him.

Amanda pulled and they entered the lounge. The room was high-ceilinged, the colours beige with a floral three-piece suite with matching curtains. A portrait of Daniel hung over the fireplace, and this surprised Jenna.

Seeing this, Susan whispered, 'It's his father,' with a smile on her face.

'Come on, Mummy!' Amanda pulled Jenna forward, just as Charlie passed them. He did not even acknowledge Jenna, but went to claim Penny.

Susan smiled at Amanda's enthusiasm.

'I want Jenna to meet Daddy,' said Amanda.

'I expect she already has,' said Susan, and again Jenna heard resignation in her hostess's voice.

She derived comfort from the small hand still in her own. Children always accepted her. They had no need to fear that she would steal their husbands away.

Jenna suspected that that was not Susan White's problem. Richard would not leave his wife because he loved Amanda—that Jenna had observed. But it did not prevent him from dallying. Susan could not know that

Jenna had no intention of encouraging Richard. She would just see an extremely attractive woman to whom men would flock.

It saddened Jenna, but she smiled and said, 'Yes, I've met your father.' Her brown eyes looked straight and true into Susan's blue ones.

A smile of great sweetness spread over the whole of Susan White's face, banishing the resignation and underlying sadness. 'We'll be friends,' she said spontaneously.

Jenna could have wept. Susan had seen the real Jenna, the vulnerable girl who had had to battle with sexual harassment and accept the suspicion and envy of other women. Susan had seen the courage and refinement which nothing could destroy. She also saw a reserve which held Jenna, the real Jenna, aloof from men. She's like Daniel, she thought.

Jenna had few female friends, and they always seemed relieved when she moved away. Even Penny was not averse to viewing Jenna with bitterness. Hadn't Penny just recently cast that, 'Oh, it's all right for you. You've only got to snap your fingers and the men fall at your feet,' at her?

Jenna grinned. 'Yes, we will.'

Amanda had been turning her head from one adult to the other, listening to the tone of their voices.

'Oh, good,' she said. Both women laughed.

'What's the joke?' Richard had come up to them unnoticed.

'This is Jenna, Mummy's friend.' The blind eyes looked in the direction of Richard's voice.

'And will you be my friend too?' His voice was thick with innuendo as he put his arm round Jenna's waist.

Jenna was shocked into answering, 'No!' The word came out more loudly than she meant, and heads turned.

His blatant approach banished Jenna's previous intention of not alienating Daniel's brother. Normally she would have deflected his unwelcome advance diplomatically, but this time her fondness for the child and her rapport with Susan made Richard's attentions even more offensive.

Her sharp rejoinder upset Amanda, who started to cry. Bending quickly, Susan put an arm round her daughter, while Richard, embarrassed by Jenna's rebuff, grabbed her hand and pulled her away.

'Did you have to make such a fuss?' he demanded, anger making his face flush.

Jenna was furious. They were standing beside a table on which glasses and drinks were laid out.

'Drink?' Richard gestured towards the bottles, hoping that the guests' attention would thus be drawn from them.

'White wine, please.' Jenna could hardly speak, she was so angry, but she needed something to steady her.

Richard's eyes ran over her figure as he handed her the wine. 'Why the brush-off?' he smiled. 'You were friendly enough when we first met. No need to behave like a little virgin.' The smile had gone from his face and his tone was sneering. 'Not with a face and figure like yours,' and his eyes widened with desire.

Jenna took a sip of her drink to moisten her dry mouth, then she snapped, 'How dare you speak to me like that?' in a fierce whisper. 'Have you no respect for your wife?'

'Oh, you'd have welcomed my advances if my wife hadn't been present?' His words were doubly offensive, and she would have slapped his face if they had not been amongst so many people.

'What's wrong with Amanda?' Daniel had approached them unseen.

'Your new nurse upset her.' Richard's tone was harsh. 'I was just telling her off.' His face was stiff with dislike. 'You know how some good-looking people can't stand the disabled.'

He looked so righteous with the evening light touching his fair hair, which was almost the colour of Daniel's, that Jenna could have wept. She was sure Daniel would believe him.

'Were you unkind to Amanda?' Daniel's tone was even, without expression, so that she could not tell what he was thinking.

She had been so disgusted by Richard's behaviour that she longed to tell Daniel the truth, but her experience with men in the past had been that they supported each other against her, so she said quietly, with her head up, 'Does what I say matter?' the bitterness in her voice reflected in her face.

But the light which had smiled kindly on Richard left Jenna's face in the dark, so that the nuances of her expression were lost. The bitterness in her voice Daniel chose to ignore, preferring to think her words insolent, and even as he did so he despised himself, because it was his attraction for her that was forcing him to deny his integrity, and for this he blamed Jenna.

'Insolence is not an admirable trait in a nurse,' he said coldly.

Jenna's jaw dropped, but, before she could defend herself, Elaine joined them.

'Darling!' she said, slipping her arm through Daniel's.

He turned to his fiancée, and Jenna took this opportunity to slip away. She could feel Richard's eyes following her.

The rest of the guests were doctors with their wives from the other practices, along with their nurses. Jenna was aware of the interest she excited among the males in the room, but she ignored it. Susan left a group of people and hurried towards her.

'What did Daniel say? He looked furious!' Her eyes were anxious.

Jenna's smile lifted the sombreness from her face.

'Nothing I can't handle,' she quipped.

Susan smiled. 'I should think there's very little you can't cope with,' she said with admiration.

Jenna grinned, 'Not much.' But it wasn't true. She was not handling her emotions where Daniel was concerned very well.

If he asked her to go to bed with him this minute she would. Just the thought was enough to make her skin burn.

To direct the conversation away from Daniel, she said, 'I'm sorry if I upset Amanda.'

'You didn't for long. Look at her!' Susan gestured towards her daughter, who was talking to one of the wives from the other practice. 'She adores her father, as I do.' The face she turned to Jenna's held pain mixed with resignation.

Jenna did not know what to say. She could not very well say, You don't need to worry about me, I won't be a threat to your happiness, for she sensed that Susan did not want put into words what Jenna suspected had happened in the past, so she just smiled.

They were standing a little apart from the other guests. Jenna saw Daniel approaching and made to move away, but Susan caught her arm.

'You must come for coffee,' she said, and Jenna heard the pleading note in her voice, but before she could reply Daniel had reached them.

'Apologising?' He was looking at Jenna, his face expressionless.

Jenna was quick, she could see the puzzlement in Susan's eyes, saw the other woman's lips form the words, What for? and, to save her new friend being placed in a position where she would have to choose between betraying her husband, if she told Daniel the truth, and thereby saving Jenna, or keep silent, Jenna said, 'Yes, I've apologised for making Amanda cry.'

Susan's eyes rounded, and this puzzled Daniel. He was puzzled even further when he saw the look of gratitude she gave Jenna, but, before he could analyse it, he felt a tug at his hand. It was Amanda.

'Why doesn't Jenna want to be my daddy's friend? One of those ladies. . .' she pointed in a general direction '. . . said he had his arm round her. I heard her, so he must have been nice.'

Amanda's small voice fell like a grenade. Daniel could no longer hide from himself what he had suspected—that Richard had lied. He realised now why Amanda had cried. Jenna had not been unkind to his niece. It was Richard to whom she had been unkind, and he was furious with his brother for deceiving him.

He turned to Jenna. 'It appears I'm the one who should apologise.' But his face was tight. It would not do for him to relax his guard, for if he did. . .

A tug of his hand saved him. 'Uncle Daniel?'

A smile swept the stiffness from his face and he crouched down beside Amanda, putting his arm about her.

'I don't think Jenna meant it quite like that.' He glanced up at the girl who was looking down at him so seriously. 'Did you, Jenna?'

His eyes were pleading, which annoyed Jenna. Did he think her so lacking in compassion as to say, Yes, I did?

She tried to hide the hurt in her eyes, but he saw it, and it aggravated him. This woman was forever making him take a look at himself, and what he saw he did not like. That she was just the instrument, and quite blameless, irritated him further, but the aggravation was with himself, not against her.

Jenna did not know this. All she saw was the hardening of his eyes. She crouched down on the other side of Amanda, almost level with Daniel, so close he could smell her perfume. It was one he had bought for Elaine, but she had not liked it, claiming it was too exotic. But it suited Jenna and excited Daniel as it never had when worn by his fiancée.

Jenna wished Daniel had risen as she had crouched, for his nearness was unsettling her. When she put her arm round Amanda below his, his sleeve touched her bare flesh, and it roused longings she had never known before.

She glanced at him, sure he would know how she was feeling, but his expression was cool, even cold.

'Of course I didn't,' she said with a smile which was reflected in her voice and reassured the child, who smiled in return.

Daniel stood up, but Jenna remained crouched and gave Amanda a hug. By the time she arose, Daniel was on the other side of the room talking to Elaine.

'Thanks,' whispered Susan, gratitude in her smile.

'Any time,' Jenna smiled. 'We nurses aim to please,' she joked.

Susan laughed, and it was this carefree sound that drew Daniel's attention. It wasn't often he heard his sister-in-law laugh these days, and he was grateful to Jenna, and glad he could be genuine in this and not look for faults in this nurse who so disturbed him.

Shortly afterwards, Daniel called for silence.

'Fill up your glasses, please.' There was a flurry to the drinks table.

Daniel drew Muriel to his side, and smiling affectionately at her said, 'Here's to a happy retirement, Muriel,' and raised his glass.

'Hear! Hear!' came from the guests as they toasted Muriel, who blushed and made to move away after a whispered 'Thank you'.

'Oh, no, you don't!' Daniel had her by the arm. He looked at the faces turned to his. 'I want to express my personal gratitude, and that of my brother, for all Muriel has done for the patients and ourselves over the years. I hope her successor will be as able.'

All eyes turned to Jenna, the men's smiling, the women's suspicious.

'No one could have had a more trustworthy helper or as clever a diagnostician.' Here they all laughed, and Muriel blushed. 'Her experience helped me over a hurdle or two, I can tell you, when I first joined the practice!

'We doctors don't appreciate enough what our nurses do for us, uncomplainingly,' here Daniel's eyes rested on Jenna for a moment. Was it in apology? she wondered, 'quietly,' he was looking at Muriel as he spoke, 'and without fuss. Secretly, I have to confess that they run the practice.' This raised a laugh. 'So please, ladies and gentlemen, raise your glasses once more to a great lady.'

There were tears in Muriel's eyes.

After the speech the guests gathered around Muriel. Jenna thought this would be a good time to leave, so she approached Susan.

Richard was standing with his wife. They were close together and yet apart, like strangers. Only her eagerness to leave drove Jenna to say goodbye, while Richard was standing there.

'Thank you for inviting me,' she said, smiling at Susan, but aware of the barely concealed desire that flared in Richard's eyes and cringing because of it.

Susan smiled, but before she could speak, her husband said, 'Allow me to see you out,' and had taken Jenna's arm before she could protest.

The brightness of the day had turned to thunder. Rumbles could be heard above the conversation as they left the room. The panelled hall was made even darker as the light from the fanlight was dimmed by the clouds.

Richard's hand was still on Jenna's arm. She pulled, but his hand tightened, and he swung her towards him, his other arm encircling her. Before she could protest, his lips came down on hers in a crushing kiss. Anger gave her strength and she wrenched her face away, but he was too strong and she could not escape from his embrace.

'Don't tell me you didn't enjoy that—your sort always do.' Jenna could feel his hot breath on her face, hear the sneer in his voice.

'And your sort always takes advantage!' she retorted, hate in her eyes.

It wasn't until the words left her lips that she realised they sounded as if she was agreeing. If only she hadn't started with, 'and'!

'Richard!'

Daniel's irate voice did what Jenna had been unable to—it broke Richard's hold.

A clap of thunder followed by a flash of lightning illuminated the hall, revealing the anger on Daniel's face, the guilt, quickly concealed, on Richard's and the defiance on Jenna's.

'She led me on,' said Richard smoothly. 'Her sort always does.' He shrugged and raised an eyebrow.

Had Daniel heard her reply to these same words that Richard had used? Jenna decided that he must have done when he said, 'I think you'd better go, Miss Reid,' in a cold voice, opening the front door for her.

It was raining heavily, but Jenna did not care. She stepped out, her back straight, her head held high. Within moments she was soaked. Her dress clung to her body, outlining its curves. The two men watched, one lustfully, the other fighting an unwelcome desire.

Tears warmed the rain's coldness on her cheeks. Damn all men! she thought as she dripped her way along the pavement, clutching her bag. Why couldn't it have been Daniel who had pulled her into his arms and kissed her? Why did he have to be engaged? Her spirits were so low—she could only think of him being out of reach. He might have given me an umbrella, she muttered miserably to herself.

Water from a car driven too close to the pavement swished over her legs. She stopped and glared at it. It slowed, then reversed. That's all I need, Jenna fumed, a kerb-crawler, and prepared to run.

'Jenna!' Daniel's voice halted her in mid-stride. His face was framed in the open window, and rain dropped tears on to his upturned face. 'Get in.' It was an order, spoken brusquely. She looked like an attractive waif, with her large, soulful brown eyes, her hair clinging wet to her head. It accentuated the wide cheekbones, the sensual mouth.

He threw open the passenger door, and rain splashed on the sleeve of his grey suit.

'I'll make your car wet,' she said, her eyes fierce. She wasn't going to listen to a lecture from him.

'Oh, for goodness' sake, stop acting like a child and get in!' Exasperation clipped his words.

Jenna squelched into the seat beside him.

'Fasten your seatbelt,' he said roughly. 'You're staying at Penny's, I gather?' The water swished on to the pavement as he moved off.

'Yes.' Jenna held herself stiffly until she felt a drip on the end of her nose and lifted her hand to catch it.

A white handkerchief appeared in front of her.

'Thanks,' she said, her tone ungracious.

She pulled down the sunguard and looked at her reflection. Black tears of mascara gave her the appearance of a white clown. She would have laughed if she had not been so miserable.

As she wiped away her dampness, she waited for Daniel's complaints. When he did not speak, she glanced at his profile. It was like a sculpture in stone. Light and shade sharpened his face, refining it. Jenna longed to touch it, break its immobility, see it smile, frown—anything except this stiffness.

'Damn!' The lights had changed to red, and Jenna breathed again.

Daniel's hands were tight on the wheel and his body was tense. She had the impression that he was eager to reach the flat and that this hold-up at the lights was annoying him.

He did not speak as they drove off, and she certainly wasn't going to.

He stopped on the river side of the flats. The swans were white against the dark water. Jenna had her hand on the door-handle, and was about to thank him when he said, 'I'd like to apologise for Richard.'

His words were so unexpected that she could only stare at his profile. He turned to face her. Jenna's eyes were luminous in the darkened interior of the car. She was the most beautiful, vibrant woman he had ever seen, but he was in love with Elaine. Jenna just stirred his baser instincts. Taking a deep breath, he added, 'Richard's inclined to forget himself sometimes.' His voice was stiff. He had not wanted to chase after her, but he had heard her retort to his brother, 'And your sort always takes advantage!' He knew, to some extent, that it was true. That Jenna attracted men was undeniable, but that she had deliberately lured his brother, Daniel doubted, and he wanted to give her the benefit of the doubt.

Jenna was aware of what it must have cost him to say these words. She recognised the pride in him, for it was in herself. Was it a sign of a softening towards her that had made him rush after her with this apology?

The hope that was rising in her heart was quenched when he said, 'I didn't want you to get the wrong impression of Richard. He has his problems, but they don't affect his work.'

So he was only defending his brother. In her bitterness, she replied, 'I understand his problem only too well.' Her eyes were as black as a moonless night. Stories of Italian vendettas slipped crazily into Daniel's mind, so that he said, before the foolishness of his words struck him, 'I hope you won't hold this aberration against him.'

Jenna was furious. 'Aberration?' Her dark eyes flashed. 'Is that how you see your brother's unwelcome advances?' Her lip curled.

She was magnificent in her anger, and he wanted to pull her into his arms, kiss her roughly, dominate her. His skin paled as he fought to control his passion.

She wrenched open the door and fled from the car before he had recovered himself enough to speak.

CHAPTER FOUR

JENNA fed her disappointment in Daniel to her love for him and hoped it would kill it. To some extent she succeeded. Her new job helped. Gradually the patients became used to her, transferring their affection from Muriel to Jenna when they found the new nurse was as kind and supportive as their old one.

Mrs Green's leg took a while to heal, but eventually Jenna was able to discharge her.

'I'll miss you, Nurse,' Emma told her, handing her a box of chocolates. 'I've enjoyed seeing your cheerful face.'

Elaine was not there, and Jenna had only seen her once. After thanking Emma for the chocolates, Jenna could not stop herself from saying, 'Is your niece expected this weekend?'

'Yes.' Emma gave her a sympathetic look. 'She's a buyer for an international fashion house,' and she mentioned its name. Jenna was impressed. 'She works mostly in London and comes here whenever she can.'

Mrs Ledson had been to the diabetic clinic. 'It was very kind of Nurse Thomas to take me,' she said. 'They're very pleased with me, especially at how clean my feet are. They're writing to Dr Daniel to ask the chiropodist to come more frequently.'

Mr Robinson, when he returned from the hospital, accepted Jenna's explanation for her behaviour that day.

Her relationship with her flatmate was strained, and Jenna resolved to move as soon as she could find a place of her own.

She did not see much of Richard, as Penny was his nurse and Jenna only had to deal with him on her colleague's days off. He was polite enough, though she sensed that it was an effort, and caught him looking at her with a mixture of dislike and lust on a couple of occasions.

Daniel treated her professionally. She addressed him as Dr White and he her as Sister Reid.

A month after Jenna's arrival, she was sitting with Susan in the café of one of the big department stores' restaurant. Jenna thought her friend was looking tired. Penny had told her that Richard had been in a bad humour for the past few days, short with the patients and with her.

'Do you find looking after Amanda tiring?' Jenna asked.

Susan frowned as she thought. 'Frustrating rather than tiring,' she said. 'I wish I could help her more, and when there are other. . .' She stopped abruptly, and Jenna knew she had just prevented herself from mentioning Richard.

They were sitting at a table by the window. The restaurant was on the top floor overlooking Swansford. Jenna could just see the river that ran through the town.

She was wearing a blue sleeveless summer dress with a boat neckline that showed off her light tan. Her hair had grown and she had brushed it behind her ears, but the short pieces on top of her head sat in a crown of curls. Her lack of make-up, instead of muting her beauty, drew attention to it.

There was a silence between them for a moment, each thinking her own thoughts. Then Susan said,

'I can't thank you enough, Jenna, for all the help you've given me.'

Jenna, who had been forming a picture of Daniel's face out of the few clouds in the sky, drew her mind from her misery and smiled.

'I haven't done anything,' she shrugged.

Susan brushed a crumb of cake off the tablecloth on

to her hand and carefully placed it on her plate. Then, looking straight into Jenna's eyes, she said, 'I seem to get strength from your calmness.'

Calmness! thought Jenna. I must be putting on a good act, for she knew just how she was anything but calm inside.

Only the other day she had seen Daniel in this very shop with Elaine. They had been at the jewellery counter. Jenna had paused behind a display of cosmetics, pretending to be interested in the product so that she could watch them. She had known it would give her pain, but she could not help herself. She was close enough to hear Elaine say, 'Oh, Daniel, it's lovely! You really shouldn't,' as she'd admired a brooch he was buying for her.

And close enough to hear his reply, 'No lovelier than you.'

Lovelier than you! Jenna had thought with derision. She had seen the acquisitiveness in Elaine's eyes. There was a hardness about the woman that Daniel did not seem to see. Suddenly she had been sorry for Daniel, and the love she had fought so hard to deny flooded back stronger than ever.

I won't let that. . . She had been going to use the word 'bitch', but felt it was not strong enough to describe Elaine. That—that. . .

'Madam!' An irate voice had drawn Jenna's attention away from the couple. 'You've burst it!' the assistant was saying.

Jenna had glanced down at the large tube of foundation she had been twisting in her agitation. It had split and was all over her hands.

'You'll have to pay for it.' The assistant's face had been stiff with disapproval.

Jenna had seen the funny side of the situation and tried to suppress her smile, but was not successful. Her face had broken out into a large grin, which angered the assistant further.

'It's no laughing matter,' she had said tartly.

Jenna's face had straightened, but her eyes still twinkled. 'No, of course it's not, and of course I'll pay.' She had drawn her purse from her shoulder-bag. 'How much is it?' The make-up on her fingers was marking her bag.

Slightly mollified, the girl had handed her a tissue. Thanking her, Jenna had wiped her hands and paid for the foundation.

The assistant had put it into a bag and handed it to her. Jenna had then glanced over to the jewellery counter before she moved away, but Daniel and his fiancée had gone.

'Well, thanks.' She was a little embarrassed now, and to change the subject she said to Susan, 'You don't know where I can find a flat, do you?'

'As a matter of fact I do.' Susan raised her eyebrows. She knew her friend shared with Penny. 'My brother's in Canada—he's a mining engineer—but he has a flat here and I lease it for him. The present tenants move out in two days' time. Would you like to see it?'

Jenna leaned forward, almost upsetting her empty coffee-cup in her eagerness. 'Rath-ther!' Her eyes were shining.

Susan smiled. 'I think you'll like it. It's in the old part of town, near the shopping centre, but overlooking the river.' Then she frowned. 'The rent's a bit steep, though,' and she told Jenna what it was.

'Oh, that's fine,' said Jenna.

They arranged a time satisfactory to them both and rose to leave. 'When do you want me to move in?' Jenna asked. 'I haven't told Penny I was thinking of finding a flat yet.'

'If you like the flat, any time that suits you. I'll just

be glad to know it's in good hands.' Susan frowned. 'It's quite a responsibility finding a suitable tenant.'

Jenna told Penny about Susan's offer when her friend came in that evening, and she was saddened when Penny accepted the move without demur, but at the same time she was relieved.

Two evenings later Jenna viewed the flat. It had an entrance hall, a large lounge with a bay window, two bedrooms of a decent size, a bathroom and a kitchen large enough to eat in. The décor and the carpets were of a neutral colour, the furniture a bit old-fashioned, but of good quality. The three-piece suite was in dark beige Dralon, comfortably arranged around a coffee-table in front of a living-flame gas fire.

It was so restful after Penny's colour scheme that Jenna took it immediately.

Susan laughed. 'Do you always make up your mind so quickly?'

'Sometimes. I know a good deal when I see one,' and she grinned.

'When our parents died, our home broke up and we each took the pieces of furniture that we wanted,' Susan told her. 'As I was already married with a home of my own, my brother Robert had first choice.' She ran a hand over the walnut sideboard. 'It brings back memories.'

Jenna heard the wistfulness in her voice and said impulsively, 'You can come here any time you want to,' adding, 'Why don't you have a key? I'll need to leave one with somebody in case I lock myself out anyway, and who better?'

'Can I really come here when you're out?'

It upset Jenna to hear the eagerness in Susan's voice. 'Of course you can.' She hastened to reassure her friend. 'It can be your refuge.'

Susan read the double meaning behind Jenna's words and impulsively gave her friend a hug.

'It's so nice to have someone who understands without having to explain,' she told her.

The thought of having a place of her own lifted Jenna's spirits, so that she hummed as she worked the next day.

'Happy, Nurse?' Jenna was giving Mr Robinson his bath. As he was a bit breathless, she had decided to chair-bath him instead.

She smiled her reply and said, 'Do you find it less stressful my washing you all over in the chair?'

'Oh, yes!'

Jenna applied Conotrane cream to his shoulder-blades and down the knobbles of his spine, noting any red areas as she did so. 'And what about you?' she asked. 'How are you feeling?'

'Not so bad.' He smiled. 'Tom's got a job. It's only as a lollipop whatsit, but it brings in some money and boosts his morale.'

'That's great.' Jenna slipped Mr Robinson's vest over his head, then gave him a rest before helping him into his shirt.

She had his feet in a bowl when the bell rang, and she was just washing between his toes when Daniel came into the room.

'Carry on, Nurse,' he said, and Jenna had an insane desire to giggle; it sounded like the *Carry On* series! The smile was on her face as she raised it to his, and he, guessing what she was thinking, grinned in return. It was the first time they had been at ease with each other since Muriel's retirement party.

'They made a film called that, didn't they?' said Mr Robinson, putting their thoughts into words.

'Yes, they did,' said Daniel and Jenna at the same time.

Daniel's guard slipped. He looked down at Jenna, sitting at the patient's feet, her face flushed, her eyes laughing into his, the white plastic apron bright against her blue dress, and the desire he had suppressed for so long flared in his eyes.

It lasted but a moment, but Jenna had seen it, and hope rose in her heart. She knew it was a vain hope, for her experience in the past had shown her that married or engaged men only wanted to use her. She had been here a month now, and if Daniel had felt more than just desire she would have known it. So she bent her head and carried on washing Mr Robinson's feet, glad she had an excuse to hide the misery she knew must be showing in her eyes.

Daniel coughed to clear the tightness in his throat.

'Well, how are you, Harry?' he asked. But the desire for Jenna could not be cleared as easily as his throat. It was there in the heat of his body, the flush in his face.

'Coming along nicely, thanks. Nurse has been very good to me. It's nice to find someone with her understanding. I expect having a mother with this complaint helps.'

Daniel's reply of, 'Yes, I can see how that must be,' sounded faint to his ears. He understood now why Jenna had acted as she had when Harry Robinson had had his bad attack.

Jenna had just finished slipping on Harry's socks and had risen. Daniel handed her a pair of trousers from the couch beside him.

Jenna could not avoid his eyes as she took them from him, but she was well in control now, and was able to smile her thanks.

The flush on Daniel's face had subsided, but, adept as he was at concealing his feelings, there still lingered a longing in the depth of his eyes that Jenna chose to ignore.

Daniel supported Harry as Jenna pulled up the trousers. The three of them were close enough for Jenna to see the interest in Daniel's eyes reflected in Harry's, and she grinned.

'You sure are a great looker, Nurse,' said Harry, a slight wheeze accompanying his words, his face smiling.

It was said respectfully, and her smile widened.

'Thanks, Mr Robinson. It's always nice to receive a genuine compliment.' She had emphasised the word 'genuine', and Daniel blushed.

'Perhaps we could have Harry's shirt off, please, Sister,' he said, his tone sharper than he intended.

He must be more careful in future to distance himself from Jenna. She was right—it was lust he was feeling, not love—how could it be otherwise?—and he conjured up Elaine's face in his mind's eye, but was alarmed when it only appeared faintly.

Jenna undid Mr Robinson's shirt and lifted it with his vest, for Daniel to sound his chest.

'Not too bad,' he said, and Jenna re-buttoned her patient's shirt. 'I'll just repeat your prescription.'

Jenna lifted the bowl of water from the floor.

'Allow me.' Daniel opened the lounge door, an urge to be near her stronger than his resolve to keep away.

It was as if there were two Daniels—the one faithful to Elaine, the other craving Jenna. It would tear him apart if he did not do something about it.

'Thank you, Doctor.' Jenna hoped the cool professionalism of her address would keep Daniel in his place. Much as she longed for him and as she suspected he longed for her, she was not going to be used—not by him—not by anyone. Her previous thought that she would run to him if he snapped his fingers was no more.

Seeing her coldness, Daniel's eyes narrowed. This woman was a professional flirt, smiling at him one minute, cold the next.

Elaine's face became stronger in his mind as he left the house, his desire for Jenna successfully quenched. So why did his hand tremble as he put the key into the ignition?

As Jenna continued on her round that morning she

wished conditions between Daniel and herself could be
relaxed and happy as it had been when they had laughed
over the *Carry On* joke. She did not dwell on this,
however. Instead she concentrated on her work and on
how she could avoid returning to the Health Centre at
eleven o'clock.

Her next patient was Mrs Dickens, the arthritic lady.
It was her bath day, and Jenna decided to bath her now
in the hope that by the time she had finished and
returned to the Health Centre, Daniel would have left
on his round.

Jenna rang the bell. There was no reply. She pressed
it again. Still no answer. She looked through the letterbox. There was nothing to see.

'Mrs Dickens!' she called. Still no reply. 'Mrs
Dickens!' Her voice was louder this time, but there was
no answer.

Jenna was very concerned. She knew Mrs Dickens
was unable to leave the flat unaided, and decided that
her patient must have fallen and knocked herself out.
Jenna had suggested that Mrs Dickens left a key with a
neighbour, but her daughter had refused.

'You can't trust the people round here, they'd rob
you blind,' she declared.

Jenna glanced at her watch. It was ten-forty-five, and
Mrs Dickens' daughter would be at work. Jenna looked
at the card in her hand. The number was there. She
knocked on the neighbouring doors in the hope that one
of the occupants had a phone, but there was no reply.
Then she remembered seeing a phone-box on the other
side of the road.

The flat was on the sixth floor, but the lift, Jenna
knew, was out of order. She hurried down the stairs,
slipping on the bottom step in her haste, but, managing
to right herself, shot out of the building.

The traffic was heavy and she had to wait for a break
in it. Eventually she dashed across the road, and by the

time she stepped into the phone-box she was hot with anxiety and the speed with which she had hurried. When she discovered that the phone had been vandalised, she punched the glass.

The nearest phone she could think of was at the Health Centre. So she dashed between the traffic and into her car. Within minutes she was driving into the car park, had left her car and was speeding through the doors. Daniel was the first person she saw. He was at the reception desk.

'I must use the phone!' The urgency in her voice alerted Daniel.

'What's happened?' he demanded.

'Oh, Daniel!' It was the first time she had used his Christian name. It was the measure of her urgency and his alarm increased.

She was so glad to see him that the reserve she usually greeted him with was not there. She did not see him as her loved one, she saw him as someone who would help her without hesitation. That he was a doctor was on the credit side.

'I couldn't get into Mrs Dickens's. . .' And she told him what had happened. 'This was the only place I could think of to phone her daughter to get the key.' Her volatile nature fought the professional discipline she had had to use throughout her nursing career to control her excitability, but she managed to conquer it. It only showed in how her words ran into each other.

'You've got the daughter's number?' Daniel's voice was calm. At her nod, he said, 'Come to my surgery, we can phone her from there.'

It was then, with the use of the word 'we', that Jenna's emotional involvement where he was concerned came to the fore, and she longed for it to be so.

Daniel held the door open for her to precede him. The last time she had been in this room was to answer Mrs Johns' accusation.

'Sit down.' He pointed to the patient's chair, but she was too agitated and preferred to stand. She leant forward over the desk, her hands clasping its edges as he dialled the number.

He was through in a moment. 'May I speak to Miss Dickens, please?' The calmness of his voice, while quietening Jenna, did nothing to steady her pulse, which seemed to gallop into her throat at his nearness.

'Miss Dickens?' Daniel waited for confirmation that it was the patient's daughter, but found it difficult to keep his mind on the emergency. All the riotous thoughts he had had about Jenna chased each other in his mind. He had to drag himself back when Miss Dickens replied in the affirmative. 'My nurse. . .'

Ah, if only I were really his nurse! Jenna's eyes softened unwillingly. Her passionate nature could no longer be denied, and it showed in the warmth of her expression, the yearning in her eyes.

Desire flared in Daniel's as he looked at her over the receiver. He leant closer, and she to him, so that only the phone's receiver separated them.

'My nurse. . .' he had to repeat himself and fought to control the tone of his voice, which threatened to roughen '. . . visited your mother this morning to give her her bath, but was unable to get a reply. We're worried that your mother might have fallen.' He did not say that he feared Mrs Dickens might be lying uncon- sious. 'If you could come right away to the flat with the key——'

He was interrupted. Jenna saw the concern on his face slip away, to be replaced by anger.

'She's away?' His eyes blazed as they looked at Jenna, who rapidly went over, in her mind, all the messages she had received in case she had forgotten that Mrs Dickens's daughter had let her know, but she was sure she had not received one, and was relieved Daniel's anger was not directed at her.

'You forgot to inform the surgery?' he barked, his eyes wide with disbelief. 'Do you realise that your neglect to tell us that your mother is staying with her sister could have resulted in our asking the police to break into your house if we hadn't been able to contact you?' His words were clipped. He looked at Jenna's astonished face as he listened to the apologies on the other end of the line.

'See that you do in future, Miss Dickens,' he said, his tone severe, before he replaced the receiver. 'That gave her a fright!' He smiled at Jenna. 'She'll let you know her mother's every move in future.'

Their faces were so close that Jenna could see the perspiration on his top lip. She wiped it away gently with her finger, her touch like a breath.

Holding her eyes with his, Daniel rose and came round the desk to take her swiftly into his arms. His lips came down on hers in a kiss, gentle at first, but then a taste was not enough. The passion, the desire he had suppressed rose blind in its force, blind to everything except that she was here in his arms.

Jenna's passion matched his. It was so great that she felt her senses leaving her. Neither of them heard the phone. Then its insistent ringing pulled Daniel's lips from hers; his breathing was rapid and harsh. He had to pause a moment after lifting the receiver to collect himself, his other arm supporting Jenna, his eyes still wide with desire.

The voice on the other end of the line came between them. It could not have had a more shattering effect if it had been a bomb. It was Elaine.

'Daniel? Is that you?' Her voice was uncertain.

He had been so swamped by his passion that he had not replied immediately. He had just lifted the receiver to stop the annoyance of its ringing.

His arm dropped from Jenna and she had to lean

against the desk for support while she fought to control
her emotions. Hearing Elaine's voice helped.

'Yes?' Daniel's voice was still harsh with emotion.

'Sorry, did I interrupt you with a patient?'

Guilt made Daniel answer, 'Yes.' And even as he did
so he despised himself and the unfulfilled desire for
Jenna which still held him in its clutches. He had never
been so aroused, but it was Elaine he wanted to marry,
Elaine he was in love with. Jenna's charms beckoned,
but that was all it was—sexual attraction. A small voice
deep inside him whispered, But Elaine has never fired
you like this, but he suppressed it firmly. The fact that
he had deceived his fiancée was worrying him. He could
not forgive deception in others, so how could he forgive
himself? So his, 'Yes, I'll meet the train. It'll be
marvellous to see you again so soon!' was more effusive
than normal.

Jenna felt betrayed. It was not a new sensation, but
for its happening now she felt she had only herself to
blame. She had allowed this new feeling of love to fool
her into supposing that Daniel was feeling something
other than sexual chemistry.

In despair, she heard him repeat the train time, saw
him write it down, and watched him replace the
receiver, saw his bent shoulders, his bowed head, but
could not move.

Then she sighed, and his head came up and she saw
the guilt, the regret. 'I shouldn't have taken advantage
of your anxiety over Mrs Dickens. It was unforgivable.'
A wry smile crossed his face. 'You shouldn't be so
attractive!'

'Attractive is the wrong word,' she said bluntly. 'You
want to go to bed with me—that's it, isn't it?'

She had hit the truth and he did not like it, but he
could not deny it; he had done enough deceiving.

'Yes.' His eyes were fierce.

'No strings attached, of course. Just a. . .' she paused

to lend emphasis to her words, then said, her voice bitter '. . .a fling.' Her eyes narrowed with contempt. 'You're no better than your brother!'

She swept out of the surgery. Her love for him had died.

CHAPTER FIVE

JENNA was glad she was a nurse. Her training had taught her to conceal her feelings, and, although she had trouble at times, it was standing her in good stead now. It enabled her to work professionally with Daniel. When she was in love with him, she had avoided contact with him as much as possible, but now it was different. She could look on him as just another doctor.

Daniel should have been pleased, but, perversely, it annoyed him, and he found himself waiting for her at coffee-time, looking out of his surgery window during the afternoon to catch a glimpse of her. This awareness was not there all the time, it just lay like a sleeping tiger that would pounce unexpectedly and overcome him.

Like today—Daniel was talking to Elaine in the reception area. He glanced over her shoulder at the clock. Four-thirty, Jenna's time for returning to the Health Centre, and he found himself waiting for the sound of her voice. When the time passed without her appearing, he was disappointed.

'Daniel!' Elaine's voice was sharp.

'I'm sorry,' he apologised quickly. He knew Elaine did not like his attention to be centred on anyone but herself when they were together. Suddenly it irked him.

'I expect you were thinking of a case.' Elaine's indulgence annoyed him further.

Jenna had been held up by a patient. Alice Hayes's hoist was giving trouble. The sling used to lift her was wearing and the replacement had not yet arrived. Jenna had meant to ask Penny at lunchtime to meet her at Mrs Hayes's, but her eye had caught Daniel crossing the car park, his back straight, a slight breeze lifting his hair, and she had forgotten.

The unthinkable had happened. The sling had torn just as Jenna was winding it to lift Alice Hayes from the bedpan. Fortunately Alice was only an inch suspended and had not been hurt when she dropped back on to the bedpan, but Jenna could not move her patient unaided.

'I'll have to get some help.' She smiled at Alice.

'That's all right, Nurse.' Alice smiled back. 'I'll be quite safe here. At least I can't fall in, not with hips my size,' and she laughed, and her excess fat laughed with her, wobbling as her shoulders shook.

Jenna's grin hid her anxiety. Mrs Hayes would be perfectly safe, as she had said, but Jenna didn't want her patient's pressure areas to break into sores, and Alice's weight on the commode could tear the skin.

She hurried back to the Health Centre, hoping to catch Penny, and was just in time to pass her friend driving in the opposite direction. Frantic waves of the arm were mistaken by Penny for what they seemed, a friendly wave, and she waved back, but continued on her way.

Jenna turned into the car park, hoping to catch one of the other nurses, but all their cars had gone. The only one there was Daniel's. He was holding the passenger door open for Elaine.

Seeing her tight expression as she approached him, his first thought was that it was directed at him, but the urgency of her movements, reminiscent of that other time a month ago, told him otherwise.

'Daniel!' She had continued to use his Christian name since that disastrous kiss, determined not to let it affect their professional relationship. It was as a colleague that she appealed to him now, much as she did not want to call on his help.

'Are any of the nurses in the Health Centre?' she asked, her face stiff.

'No, they've all gone. Can I help?'

He had forgotten Elaine was there until she said, 'Daniel, we'll be late,' in a plaintive voice. They were to attend a fashion show, followed by a cocktail party at a large store in a nearby town.

The last thing Jenna wanted was to have Daniel's assistance; it reminded her of that other time when she had thought Mrs Dickens was lying unconscious in her flat, and of the kiss that had followed, but she must forget her miseries and think of Alice.

'Alice Hayes's sling has broken and I can't move her on my own from the commode,' she told him.

'Well, can't you get a joiner or something?' Elaine's voice was impatient.

'It's not as simple as that, Elaine,' Daniel said in a curt way. He handed her the keys. 'Take the car. I'll see you at your aunt's as soon as I can.'

'You mean you're leaving me? Going with this nurse?' Elaine was annoyed.

'I must.' Daniel's face was stern.

'Oh, very well.' Elaine's annoyance had turned to anger. She slipped into the driving seat and slammed the door.

Jenna, with Daniel beside her, was driving out of the car park before Elaine had put her car into gear.

She had left Alice's door on the snib so that she would be able to re-enter.

'Ah, Nurse!' Alice smiled broadly at them both, quite unembarrassed by her situation. 'It's many a day since I felt a man's arms around me,' she said as Jenna and Daniel lifted her from the commode on to her chair. Jenna could not help but laugh, and Daniel grinned.

'Mmm, I love your aftershave, Dr Daniel,' said Alice, sniffing appreciatively. 'You must tell me what it's called. Make a nice spray, don't you think so, Nurse?'

Jenna looked at the grinning Daniel and laughed again.

'It's a good job you didn't say that when we were lifting you,' said Daniel, suddenly more light-hearted than he had been since he had kissed Jenna. 'We might have dropped you.'

'Oh, I have absolute faith in the power of the medical profession.'

They both glanced at Alice's straight face and laughed. The incident had relieved the tension Jenna was feeling and she felt able to ask Daniel, 'I wonder if I can impose on you further?'

Daniel's glance at his watch brought Elaine into the room. Jenna tensed, then chided herself. She did not want the sudden ease she was feeling in Daniel's company to slip away. What was it to her that he was engaged? She wasn't interested in him now.

'I wonder if you could spare the time. . .' she could not help a touch of sarcasm entering her voice '. . .to help me lift Mrs Hayes on to the bed.' She smiled down at the disabled woman. 'It'll give you another chance to put your arms around Dr Daniel's neck!'

Alice laughed.

'Well, I'm all for pretty women doing that,' Daniel surprised himself by saying, his grin including both Jenna and Alice. It was such a cheeky grin that both the women laughed, and Jenna thought, What's the point in harbouring a hurt anyway? It only sours you. And with this decision the bond about her heart snapped and she felt so relieved that she smiled easily at Daniel, all her stiffness gone.

She had been so distant with him since his kiss that her smile caught him unawares and he found difficulty in breathing for a moment.

When he did not move, Jenna asked, 'Can you help?' in a puzzled tone.

'Of course.' Daniel's reply was brisk.

He stayed until Jenna had inspected Alice's pressure areas and applied cream.

'You're doing a good job there,' he complimented Jenna on Alice's unbroken skin.

'Thank you.'

Her smile was as natural as he could have wished, and he should have been pleased that the stiffness between them had gone, but he wasn't. It signified a lack of interest in him as a man, and this should have pleased him, but it didn't.

As he helped Jenna move Alice from the bed to the wheelchair, his awareness of Jenna, which he thought he had successfully suppressed since their kiss, flared again. Her hair touched his face, her hand touched his, her. . .

'I think you deserve a cup of tea,' said Alice Hayes, smiling, after they had settled her.

'Thanks, but I have an appointment,' Daniel told her.

'And I must drive the doctor to it,' said Jenna, smiling. 'Your daughter will be in soon. The evening staff will bring a sling from one of the other health centres tonight when they come.'

'Thanks, Nurse. Thanks, Dr Daniel.'

Alice was still in their minds as they took their seats in the car. 'You'd never think she lost her husband last year,' Daniel remarked, clipping on his seatbelt. 'She never lets you see the pain.'

'No.' Jenna's tone was thoughtful. 'There are many people like that.' She was glad her painful love for Daniel had died. 'I take it you'd like me to drop you at Mrs Green's?'

'Thanks.'

He seemed to fill the Mini, and Jenna wished Alice had not drawn attention to his aftershave. Jenna had been unaware of it before, but now it. . . Would she ever be able to rid herself of the scent of it in her car?

They did not speak as they drove the short distance to Emma Green's. 'Thanks for the lift,' Daniel said over his shoulder as he stepped from the car.

'Any time,' she said with a smile.

She was reversing the car. Mrs Green came out of the house before Daniel had reached the door.

'Elaine said she couldn't wait, and she took your car.' Her expression was apologetic.

Jenna had her window down, so she heard Emma's words and also heard Daniel's, 'Damn!'

'Looks as if "any time" is now,' she called, leaving the car to join them. 'How are you, Mrs Green?'

'Very well, thanks. I miss your cheery visits, though.'

Jenna grinned. 'I'm sure. . .' she could not bring herself to speak Elaine's name '. . .your niece comes as often as she can.'

'Oh, yes,' Emma agreed, too quickly, and Jenna was sorry for the lonely old lady.

When they were seated in the car, she asked Daniel where he would like to go.

'Home,' he said. There was a weariness in his voice.

Compassion for a colleague made Jenna say, 'I'm sorry if I spoiled your evening.' Then impulsively, seeing the tired lines on his face, she said, 'Would you like to come home with me for a bite to eat? I've got a chicken in the slow cooker. I was thinking of making it into a risotto.'

He knew he should not accept her offer, but he was very hungry. It was now six o'clock and he had only had a sandwich lunch. He was annoyed with Elaine for taking his car and going without him. Daniel knew she was ambitious, but surely she could have missed this show, which led him to say, 'I'd like that. If you stop at a wine shop or a supermarket, I'll provide the drink.'

Jenna smiled and did as he requested. They were soon at the flat.

'I heard you took over Robert's flat,' he remarked as she let them in.

An appetising smell greeted them. 'Hmm, that smells good,' he said, passing her the bottle of wine.

The lounge was the same as he remembered it, and yet there was a subtle difference about it—Jenna's personality was everywhere. He would have thought the neutrality of the décor would have irked her, and that she would have filled the room with vibrant colours, but, except for a picture of Spanish dancers over the fireplace, the colours she had added were muted—a black figure in a striking pose, a white vase full of pink roses, an occasional table in the window. Even the books on the bookshelves had quiet covers.

Jenna lit the fire to warm the room. It was this setting that showed a different side of her. There was also a new maturity about her. The amused smile, the provocative air, the tantalising swing to her hips were all gone. He saw a Jenna more beautiful than that vibrant, alive woman who had taken over from Muriel, and he wished he had not accepted her invitation.

Rain tap-tapped on the window as if it were admonishing him.

'Sit down,' Jenna gestured towards the armchair. 'It won't be long.'

The quietness of the room, two floors above the road, seeped into his weariness. He could fight no more, and he closed his eyes. He was asleep when Jenna returned. She had changed into rust-coloured trousers, matched with a blouse patterned in autumnal shades. They were colours she had never worn before, but since falling in love with Daniel, and his rejection of her, she had felt a need to change her wardrobe.

The steam rising from the risotto woke him, and he pulled himself into a sitting position. 'Sorry about that.' His face was soft with sleep; his eyes, still heavy, made him look seductive.

Jenna was sure of herself and could look at him dispassionately. She handed him the corkscrew with the wine. 'Would you do the honours, please?'

'It's the least I can do,' he smiled, and opened the

bottle, filling the two glasses she had put on the coffee-table.

But she pushed hers aside. 'Better not,' she said. 'I must run you home later on.'

'No,' he protested, pushing the glass back towards her. 'I can walk from here, it's just round the corner.'

'Oh?' She hadn't even wondered where he lived when she had been in love with him; it hadn't mattered.

Daniel ate a mouthful of risotto and took a sip of wine.

'That's marvellous,' he said, and ate some more.

Jenna was seated on the couch, her appetite as keen as his. 'What's your house like?' she asked between mouthfuls.

'It's one of the old houses. It belonged to my grandfather. He was a doctor in Swansford and we used to stay with him on our school holidays.' He drank some wine. The rain had darkened the room. Only the firelight's glow reflected on their faces and threw their shadows together. It was cosy and companionable, and Jenna did not want to turn on the lights in case it dispelled the easiness between them.

'He was a good practitioner. My father had disappointed him by choosing a banking career instead of medicine, so Grandfather did his best to influence Richard and me, with resulting success.' He smiled.

Jenna saw the attractiveness of his smile for what it was—an attractive smile. It no longer had the power to melt her bones; a small tremor deep inside her she ignored.

'He left me the house in his will. He knew I wanted to be a GP, here in Swansford. My brother he wasn't too sure about.' Daniel smiled ruefully. 'He felt Richard was more the consultant type, and in this he was right, but an early marriage followed by Amanda put paid to that.' His face became serious. 'Richard loved Amanda from the moment she was born and decided he would have more time to devote to her in general practice.' He

stared into the fire, a thoughtful expression on his face.
'I sometimes wonder if he regrets his decision.' It was
almost as if he was speaking these last words to himself,
so Jenna made no reply.

They finished their risotto in silence. 'Would you like
a sweet?' she asked as she collected the plates.

She was bending forward, her face close to his. What
beautiful eyes she has! he thought. They could be dark
and warm, or black with anger. At the moment they
were smiling.

'Cheese would be nice.'

Jenna cleared the table, refusing his offer of help
with, 'You stay by the fire and rest.'

She returned with a selection of biscuits and cheese.

'Wine?' He held the bottle over her glass.

'Just half, please.'

Daniel filled his own glass and raised it to her.

'Here's to "any time",' he smiled. 'I hope it extends
from lifts to more meals like this.'

It was meant as a joke and his voice was amused, but
his eyes, though smiling, held a touch of wistfulness,
and he could not stop himself saying, 'I've enjoyed this
evening very much.'

Jenna decided he was only being polite and replied
lightly, 'Yes, I have too,' rising with the cheeseboard.
'Coffee?' She ignored his 'any time' suggestion.

He was disappointed. Had he expected a more mean-
ingful reply? If so. . . He was not prepared to delve so
deeply inside himself for an answer. He felt guilty
enough at feeling more relaxed with Jenna than he did
with Elaine, but then love created tension, didn't it? It
was natural that he should feel like that with Elaine,
wasn't it?

Jenna's return with the coffee pushed his thoughts
aside. He drank it quickly and rose.

'Can I help with the washing-up before I go?' he
offered.

'You can't go yet.' Jenna gestured towards the rain running down the window. 'You'll get soaked!'

Daniel knew he should leave, but the cosiness of the room had warmed his bleakness and he sat down once more in the comfortable armchair.

'You cooked that risotto like an Italian. Do you have any Italian blood?' He let her pour him another cup of coffee.

Jenna laughed. 'I'm always being asked that! I had an Italian grandfather who handed down the secret.'

Daniel was interested. 'You must have relatives in Italy, then?'

She shrugged. 'I suppose so, but I've never seen them. My grandfather was an Italian prisoner of war over here, and that's how he met my gandmother. She was one of the daughters of the farmer for whom he worked. It was love at first sight. . .' A family failing, she thought, hoping her face did not betray the sadness she felt. 'After the war, he returned and married her. His family didn't approve, and disowned him.' She drank some of her coffee.

'Do you believe in love at first sight?' Daniel asked quietly.

This was too close to the truth for Jenna. She rose, bending to collect the coffee-cups to hide the pain she knew must be showing in her eyes.

'No,' she said firmly. 'It's just an old wives' tale,' and left the room without waiting for his comment.

Daniel was on his feet looking out of the window when she returned. 'The rain has stopped. I think I should go.'

The evening sun, breaking through the clearing skies, shone upon him, bathing him with its golden light, making his blond hair fairer, his blue eyes bluer. Looking into them, Jenna saw pictures of golden beaches and blue seas, and clear blue endless skies. He'll always be a golden moment for me—the thought slipped past her guard and filled her eyes with sorrow.

Daniel touched her arm. 'What is it, Jenna?' he asked, his voice sharp with concern.

'Nothing,' she said, stepping back, annoyed with herself. 'Would you like an umbrella?'

He grinned. 'I don't think a floral umbrella would suit my image, do you?'

Her tension escaped in laughter. 'No, but a plain black one?'

Daniel glanced out of the window. A few spots were falling. 'Well. . .'

'I'll fetch it.'

She was back in a moment, a smile on her face as she held the umbrella out to him handle first.

He laughed as he grasped the duck's head.

'I always feel like Mary Poppins when I use it,' she confessed, her smile broadening.

'If I put it up will it fly away with me?'

The thought of him vanishing out of her life forever was so awful that for a moment Jenna was speechless. It had been a mistake to bring him here. She could fool herself no longer. She loved this man, but her time in the wilderness had matured her, made her wary, so she smiled.

'It only flies away with magical ladies,' she told him.

'Well, you'd better not use it again.' He had seen the look in her eyes and his voice softened.

This Jenna could not take. He was doing it again— trying to seduce her, like all the others. She turned abruptly away.

'I'll see you out.' She gestured pointedly before her. The evening was spoilt.

She was about to close the door after him when he said, 'I'll see you get this back,' waving the umbrella.

Jenna wanted to shriek, Keep it! I never want to see it, or you, again, but she just nodded and closed the door.

CHAPTER SIX

JENNA managed to control her emotions and forced herself to be friendly when she had to see Daniel during the next week. As day followed day, it became easier, but she was glad he was going to be away on Monday at a GPs' meeting.

Her flat became as much a haven for herself as it did for Susan. Jenna often came home to find a thank-you note propped against a vase of fresh flowers or a box of chocolates.

On the Monday morning Daniel was away, Susan phoned Jenna before eight-thirty. 'Glad I caught you. Would you like to come for dinner this evening? I'm missing my daughter so!' Amanda was away on a holiday organised by her school.

Hearing the plaintive note in Susan's voice, Jenna accepted, 'I'd love to come,' which was true. She wanted to see Susan, but not Richard. Hoping he would not be there, she asked, 'Anyone else coming?'

'No, there'll just be the two of us—Richard will be out. Come about seven-thirty.'

Monday was a busy day. Jenna had two new cases—one a man, Michael Smith, who had broken both his legs in a traffic accident. He had been looked after by his wife, but she had fallen and broken her wrist, so was unable to wash or care for her husband. It would take time, and Jenna would have to reorganise her work accordingly.

The other case, a skin dressing, would take about an hour. The patient, a woman, had been attending the treatment-room with dermatitis of her hands, but it had

broken out on her feet, so a home visit had been
requested.

Jenna closed her eyes for a moment and sighed.

'Heavy workload?' Penny asked, as she collected
dressing packs from the cupboard.

'Let's just say you won't see me at lunchtime,' said
Jenna. 'I'll be lucky if I finish this lot by two o'clock.'

'I'd offer to take some from you, but I'm up to
here. . .' Penny put her hand to her chin '. . . myself.'

'Thanks for the offer, but I'll manage.'

The bad start to the day spread throughout the
morning. Mrs Dickens was home again and had phoned
Jenna to tell her that her daughter would leave the door
snibbed, so she wouldn't have to struggle to the door.

Jenna pushed the door open and called, 'It's only the
nurse, Mrs Dickens,' closing it carefully after her.

A groan was her answer. She hurried into the bedroom. The fear that she had had before when she could
not raise an answer that other time was now realised.
Mrs Dickens had fallen, and, by the angle of her leg,
had broken her femur.

'It was that rug, Nurse, the one you said I should
move, but I wouldn't—my husband made it.' Her face
tightened with pain. 'I caught my foot in it this morning,
just a little while ago.' She was pale with shock.

Jenna glanced at her watch. It was nine-thirty.

'Well, don't worry. I'll phone the surgery, but before
I do I'll just cover you with your duvet.'

As soon as she had made Mrs Dickens comfortable
she phoned the Health Centre and asked to be put
through to Richard. When she explained what had
happened, he said,

'Well, send for the ambulance. I don't know why
you're wasting my time. You *are* a qualified nurse, aren't
you?' and cut the line.

Oh, how I hate you! thought Jenna as she dialled for

the ambulance. While she waited for it, she phoned Mrs Dickens's daughter.

It was ten-forty-five before she left, having seen her patient into the ambulance.

She went straight to Mr Smith's.

'This won't do, Nurse,' Vera Smith, an attractive woman in her late thirties, blonde with a good figure, greeted Jenna, her tone imperious. 'My husband's always up and dressed by now.' She waved her plastered arm. 'If I hadn't broken my wrist, I would never have needed any help.'

'I'm sure the receptionist will have told you that we can't state a definite time for calling.' Jenna tried to keep the bite out of her voice, but the aggravation of Richard's words was still with her. She knew a nurse was supposed to be all 'sweetness and light', but sometimes it was impossible.

It was a cool September day, but Jenna was hot. She wished she had not put on her mac, and she removed it with relief.

'There's no need to speak to me like that!' Mrs Smith's tone was as sharp as Jenna's.

How Jenna longed to tell her of the aggravations of the morning, but she controlled herself and apologised.

'I'm sorry. I'll try and get here earlier tomorrow.'

'Well, see that you do.'

This case was going to be more difficult than she had suspected, Jenna thought. She was going to have to be very careful not to offend Mrs Smith, and she was going to have to start now.

'I'd be very grateful if you'd tell me just how your husband likes to be looked after,' she began.

Jenna had thought her tone polite and that it would mollify Vera Smith, but when that lady snapped, 'There's no need to be sarcastic!' Jenna realised that nothing she would ever say would be right. Perhaps when Mrs Smith saw that Jenna had no wish to take her husband over, and was just there to help until Vera's arm was better, she would accept Jenna, but at the moment Jenna wasn't sure, so she smiled.

'And don't think a smile like that will sweep my husband off his feet! It's been tried before.'

This was more serious. It was the real reason for Vera Smith's hostility and must be handled firmly and at once.

'Mrs Smith,' Jenna said, her face expressionless, 'I'm here to assist your husband to wash and dress, and to help him into his wheelchair. That. . .' she held Vera's eyes with her own, '. . . and only that is what I intend to do.'

Vera Smith's shoulders seemed to sag. 'That remains to be seen,' she said, her face stiff.

'If you would take me to the patient?' Jenna gestured, and Vera led her to the bedroom.

The man sitting up in bed looked out of place in a room which was essentially feminine—pink predominated. Curtains, wallpaper, bedlinen and duvet cover were all in that colour.

Jenna had expected to see a dark-haired, virile womaniser in the bed, and was surprised and relieved to find Michael Smith was a mildly handsome man, with dark hair, blue eyes, a thin build and no sexual magnetism.

But Jenna did not relax her guard. She greeted Michael Smith with a professional smile, 'Hello, Mr Smith,' and could feel Vera's eyes watching her.

Michael did smile, however, as he said, 'Hel-lo!' in a manner which did nothing to improve Jenna's standing with his wife.

Jenna ignored his tone and turned to Vera. 'If you could give me a bowl and show me where the bathroom is?'

Vera showed her, her body stiff with tension as she led the way. When they returned with the bowl of hot water, soap, facecloths and towel, Jenna said,

'Would you be kind enough to put out your husband's clothes?' knowing this was in Vera's capacity to do so with her arm in plaster.

It did not take long for Jenna to assist Michael to wash and dress, nor to transfer him to the wheelchair. Vera had remained in the room all the time, and Jenna was glad. Her behaviour with Michael was strictly professional, so Vera could not fault her.

But it was a worried Jenna who returned to the Health Centre well after eleven o'clock, for Vera Smith had remained suspicious throughout her visit.

Penny was just leaving as Jenna stepped through the doors. 'What have you done to Richard?' she wanted to know. 'He was ranting and raving about incompetent nurses!' Her eyes gleamed.

'Nothing,' Jenna sighed. 'Just asked him to visit a patient who'd fallen and broken her femur. He bawled me out and told me to send for an ambulance.'

'He certainly has it in for you, doesn't he?'

Jenna was saddened to hear the satisfaction in her friend's voice. The recent harmony between Daniel and herself was disturbing Penny, who still longed for the handsome doctor and envied Jenna.

'You won't have to contend with him, anyway.' There was a softening in Penny's expression. 'He's back in surgery.'

'That's something.' Jenna took a deep breath.

She would not admit to herself that she missed Daniel. She drank her coffee quickly. There would not have been any use discussing the problem of Mrs Smith's hostility with him anyway; he might have blamed herself.

By the time she arrived home, she was so tired that she wished she had not accepted Susan's invitation to dinner. She could have excused herself, but she knew it would disappoint Susan if she did so.

Feeling better after a soak in the bath up to her neck

in scented bubbles, she slipped into beige trousers and a cream blouse. She put on her brown leather jacket and left the flat.

Richard's car was in the drive, but Jenna was not disturbed. Someone had probably collected him; Jenna knew he was a keen badminton player.

But when Susan answered the door, Jenna's heart dropped. She knew what her friend was going to say. Susan's face was tight.

'Richard decided not to go tonight.' Susan's eyes were pleading.

'Oh!' Jenna could not think of anything else to say, and if she could, Richard might hear her. With leaden feet, she followed Susan into the lounge.

'Ah!' Richard did not even rise from his chair. 'The nursing sister.' His tone was disparaging. 'Some nurse, if you can't act on your own responsibility.'

Jenna was furious. 'It's not in my job description that I'm responsible for diagnosing the patients,' she said coldly.

'Well, she did have a fractured femur, as you suspected.' His tone was defensive. 'I phoned the hospital, so you can stop looking so disapproving.'

Probably regretted his decision not to visit, thought Jenna, turning away and ignoring him.

'Is Amanda enjoying her holiday?' she asked Susan.

The strain lifted from Susan's eyes, making her look younger. 'Yes—a super time,' she smiled. 'Would you like a drink?'

'No, thanks. I'm driving.'

'Little Miss Goody-goody!' sneered Richard.

'Come and help me in the kitchen while I tell you about Amanda,' said Susan, her face stiff with tension.

Jenna followed her with alacrity.

'I'm sorry Richard was so rude to you,' said Susan, as she checked the casserole. 'He's just jealous of you.'

'Me?' Jenna's eyebrows rose in surprise. She had

thought Richard's behaviour was because she had rejected him. 'Why?'

'Because we're friends.' Susan looked worried.

'Tough for him, then.' Jenna smiled. 'Nothing he can say will destroy my friendship for you.'

Susan was relieved. 'Thanks. I was so afraid. . .'

Jenna gave her a hug. 'Don't be. We Reids are made of stern stuff—we bend, we don't break.' The pun on her name made them both laugh.

'Are we getting any dinner tonight?' Richard's voice came from the doorway. His face was unsmiling, his eyes narrowed.

'Yes.' Susan's voice was cheerful. 'The grapefruit's ready.' And both the girls laughed, but not for any reason.

'I don't see what's funny about that.' Richard could barely conceal his anger at being left out.

'You just don't have the right sense of humour,' Jenna said boldly, then wished she hadn't when she realised how her words united herself with Susan and saw Richard's face darken.

He turned on his heel and left them.

'Perhaps I should go,' she said ruefully.

'No,' Susan said firmly. 'I invited you for dinner, and dinner you shall have.'

As the meal progressed, the atmosphere became more strained. Richard drank more and more wine.

When they had finished their sweet, Jenna rose. 'I think I should go,' she said. 'Can I help with the dishes?'

'Not staying for coffee? Tut-tut!' Richard laughed drunkenly.

'I'll do the dishes,' Susan said, trying to hold back her tears.

'Well, let me help you through with them.' Jenna lifted the collected sweet plates.

In the kitchen she said, concern in her eyes, 'Will you be all right?'

'Yes.' Susan was stiff with tension. 'He'll probably go to sleep now.' She touched Jenna's arm. 'Don't you worry. I'm just sorry your dinner was spoilt.'

'Where's the coffee?' roared Richard from the dining-room.

'Coming!' Susan called back, reaching for the coffee tray.

'I'll phone you in the morning,' Jenna promised.

'Thanks, but I'll be all right,' Susan repeated, and she sounded so positive that Jenna left the house reassured, but a niggling doubt still remained.

It was a relief to climb into her car and drive home. The flat seemed even more welcoming after the tension of the evening.

She had just finished watching a film on television and had risen to turn off the set when she heard a noise in the hall. Jenna was not a nervous girl. She snatched up a vase, threw open the lounge door and was about to say, 'If you don't get out I'll hit you with this!' when the light from the lounge showed Susan, a bruise darkening the right side of her face.

'Susan!' Jenna's voice was horrified. She rushed to put an arm round her friend and draw her into the lounge. Susan was wearing just her dress with no coat, and she was shivering. Her face was wet with tears and her eye was beginning to close.

'I didn't know where else to go,' she whispered.

Jenna lit the fire. 'You'll be all right now. I'll bring you a cup of tea.'

Susan closed her eyes and leant back in the same armchair that Daniel had sat in. 'I feel safe here,' she whispered.

Jenna was back in a few minutes with two mugs of tea and a rug which she wrapped round her friend, leaving only a hand out to hold the mug.

They sipped their tea in silence. Then Susan said, 'It was only because he'd drunk too much. He'd never have hit me otherwise.' She wrapped her hands round the mug. 'He gets like this when Amanda's away.' Her face was pathetic. 'You see, he blames himself for her blindness. He was a student, I was pregnant and Richard thought the rash I had was due to a sore throat.' She smiled tremulously. 'You know how it is—we never thought any more about it. Amanda was born blind.' Susan's expression was piteous as she looked at Jenna, and said, 'Richard blames me as well. I was training to be a schoolteacher and had been on placement. We heard about the German measles at the school later, but I didn't think anything about it until Amanda was born.' Tears filled her eyes. 'I was only there for a day.'

'But what about your immunisation against German measles at school?' asked Jenna.

'I was ill when the others had it and it got forgotten.'

'But the antenatal clinic? They test your blood.'

Susan gave a big sigh. 'I didn't tell Richard I was pregnant.' The tears flowed now. 'I knew he didn't want a child. He was ambitious.' Her eyes were full of grief. 'He wanted to be a consultant in surgery.' She paused for a moment. 'So you see, it was my fault and not his. I had to tell him eventually that I was pregnant and he was delighted, but by that time I was in my thirteenth week—too late.'

Susan would never have confided in Jenna if she had not been so distraught, and this Jenna knew, and was touched.

To say she was sorry would be too inadequate, so she just put her arms round Susan and hugged her.

It was late—midnight. A wind had risen and was breathing against the windows.

'I'll put a hottie in the spare bed and run you a bath,' said Jenna. 'You can have one of my nighties.'

'I should go back.' Susan sounded unsure.

'Leave it until the morning. Richard will have sobered up by then.' Jenna's voice was soft.

'Perhaps you're right,' Susan agreed, too tired and upset to think.

Jenna had the tray of mugs in her hand when the bell rang imperiously. Susan started to tremble and half rose.

Jenna put down the tray. 'You stay there—I'll deal with him,' she said firmly.

Susan sank back in the chair, her face fearful.

Jenna closed the lounge door quietly behind her. She put the chain on the front door and opened it. Daniel was standing elongated in the narrow opening. His expression was grim.

'Is Susan here?' His voice was abrupt.

'What makes you think she is?' Jenna's face was as grim as his.

'Well, for one thing, you're up, and, for another, Richard said this was where I'd find her. So stop beating about the bush and let me in.' His words were clipped.

'Richard isn't——?' she began.

'No, he isn't with me.'

'I'll see if she wants to see you. Women are no longer the downtrodden sex, you know. We have our rights.'

'I wasn't aware that you were a feminist?' Amusement softened the sternness of his expression.

'Hmm.' Jenna left him.

Feminist? I suppose I am, she thought, and no wonder!

Susan agreed to see her brother-in-law, so Jenna let Daniel in. He went straight to the lounge and crouched beside Susan. Taking both her hands in his, he said the words Jenna had been unable to utter. 'I'm so sorry, Susan,' and they sounded so right on his lips.

Tears ran down Susan's cheeks. Daniel whipped out his handkerchief and dabbed her cheeks, and she winced as he touched her swollen one.

'I came to see Richard to tell him the results of the meeting. I must have arrived just after you'd gone.' He took a deep breath. 'He's distraught—can't bring himself to believe that he hit you, Susan. He's threatening to kill himself.' Susan's eyes rounded with shock and she made to rise, but he pushed her gently back. 'I sedated him. I must go back right away, I only left him to find you. Will you come back with me?'

Susan's face had aged. It was pinched, the clear eyes were clouded, the unbruised cheek was pale.

'Only if Jenna can come too,' she whispered.

'I don't think that's a good idea.' Daniel glanced up at Jenna, who was standing dark and silent beside him. 'I'm afraid he blames her.'

Life returned to Susan's eyes. 'Well, I'm not coming, then,' she said firmly, then added pathetically, 'At least, not tonight.' Her face was sad. 'I'm afraid to.' It was even sadder that she felt she had to excuse herself, and Jenna felt tears in her eyes.

'Very well.' Daniel's voice was gentle. He rose to his feet.

'I'll see you out,' said Jenna, her face expressionless.

Daniel paused at the front door. 'Sometimes I wish you'd never come to Swansford. Our lives were clear and simple before then.' His face was grim.

'Were they, Dr Daniel?' Jenna said, in a quiet voice. 'Are you sure?'

Daniel had the feeling that she was not talking about Richard and Susan, but about himself.

CHAPTER SEVEN

RICHARD'S attack on his wife seemed to act as a catharsis. When Susan returned to her husband two days later, he was a changed man. The autocratic, sarcastic husband was no more, and in his place was a subdued man.

Daniel insisted that his brother took two weeks off, something Jenna was pleased to hear when she went in on Tuesday. It meant she would not have to face him, for she would not have known what to say. He blamed her.

After work on Thursday, she took a risk and phoned Susan, and was relieved when it was her friend who answered it.

'How are things?' Jenna asked.

Susan told her how Richard had changed. 'We're going away for a few days!' She sounded excited. 'I can't believe how gentle he is, Jenna.'

'That's great.' Jenna was delighted.

'He asked me to apologise to you.' There was wonderment in Susan's voice.

He certainly has changed, thought Jenna wryly, but was relieved nevertheless. 'Have a marvellous time,' she said.

'I'll phone you when we come back,' Susan promised.

'I'll look forward to that.'

Daniel too seemed to have changed. He treated Jenna with friendliness and a respect which Jenna realised had been missing before. He must have forgotten what he had said when they had parted at her flat, she thought, or perhaps he was regretting the injustice of his words.

A week later Jenna returned to the Health Centre at

eleven o'clock. She had just come from the Smiths'. Her relationship with Vera had improved slightly.

As soon as Jenna walked into the staff lounge, Daniel rose to his feet and offered to pour her coffee.

'What are you after?' she asked, an amused twinkle in her eye.

He gave a small laugh. 'Is it that obvious?'

'Only to the trained eye,' she quipped, accepting the mug from him.

They were alone. Penny was late.

'I'd like you to chaperon me,' Daniel said, sitting in his vacated seat.

Jenna sat opposite to him. 'What's it worth?' she asked boldly.

'Dinner at my place?' It was said like a challenge.

Jenna hid her surprise. 'Tête-à-tête?' Her eyebrows rose.

'Yes.' His blue eyes gleamed with amusement.

'How will Elaine like that?' Her expression was wry.

'She'll never know. It'll be our secret.' His tone was conspiratorial. 'Anyway, she's in America.'

To hide her surprise at the way the conversation was going, Jenna said, 'That's not much of a compliment to me,' but she smiled. She wanted to see his house.

'Are your feminist hackles rising?' he grinned.

'But of course.' Her smile broadened. 'I ought to refuse your offer, but I could do with a good meal, and I'd love to see your house.'

'Touché!' This time Daniel laughed aloud. 'It should be an interesting evening. Come along at seven-thirty.' And he told her his address.

They finished their coffee. As they walked to his surgery, Daniel told her about the patient.

'Mrs Frances Holden has been to see me a couple of times. She's an attractive woman in her late forties who's been divorced three times. She always comes to the surgery wearing a low-cut blouse or dress and leans forward to make sure I see her cleavage.' He sighed wearily. 'There's nothing wrong with her that I can discover—she's just lonely and searching for another husband.'

'Ah!' Jenna's eyes twinkled. 'She's lining you up.'

Daniel laughed. 'So it would appear.' Then his face became serious. 'I even feel threatened at times. Ridiculous, isn't it?'

They had reached his room, and he opened the door for Jenna to precede him.

'Now you know how I feel,' she said, a wry expression on her face.'

'Yes.' He looked at her, and it was as if he was seeing her with different eyes. 'Attractive doctors and nurses are open to abuse.' Then he grinned. 'That's why I need a chaperon.'

Jenna laughed. 'I'll take you with me on my rounds if I have to visit Mark Johns again,' she couldn't resist saying.

'I deserved that,' he said, but he smiled.

Daniel asked Shirley Gardener to send Mrs Holden in. Jenna was standing beside the couch when Frances Holden came in.

'Oh, Doctor. . .' The pathos in her voice vanished when she saw Jenna. 'What's she doing here?' Her eyes were hostile. 'I don't want anyone else to hear my symptoms.'

'Nurse is here as a chaperon, Mrs Holden.' Daniel rose. 'I'd like to give you a complete medical examination.'

Mrs Holden's eyes gleamed. 'But surely, Doctor, it would be better if Nurse wasn't present?' Her innuendo was plain.

'That's exactly why the nurse is here.' His eyes were serious. 'We must observe the proprieties.'

Jenna thought she heard Frances whisper, 'Must we?'

and glanced at Daniel, but, if he had heard, he had ignored it.

He gestured towards the couch and Jenna drew the curtain round it, leaving an opening for the patient to enter.

There was something vaguely familiar about Frances Holden that eluded Jenna. She wore a short nylon leopardskin jacket, a black fitted dress, black tights, patent leather shoes, and wore plenty of golden jewellery, at least four heavy chain necklaces and two charm bracelets. Big gold earrings hung from her ears. Her make-up was heavy and thick, her lips bright red, her eyeshadow brown, her mascara as black as her hair. The overall effect was striking. It was only as she undressed, put her clothes in a neat pile on the chair, and stood in just her black slip that she appeared to have discarded her brassiness along with her clothes.

Jenna saw a woman weary of life. The black hair was dry and brittle, just as Frances Holden was.

'Would you lie on the couch, Mrs Holden, please?' Jenna's voice was warm and gentle.

Frances Holden took a deep breath and lay down.

As she put her head back on the pillow, Jenna thought she saw tears glisten in the brown eyes. The wrinkles gathered in her neck as her chin lowered.

'Dr Daniel's very gentle,' Jenna reassured her patient.

'Yes, I'm sure he is,' Mrs Holden said wistfully.

'I'll just tell him you're redy.'

Daniel came immediately. His examination was gentle and thorough. When it was completed, he said, 'When did you last have a smear taken?'

'A smear? What's that?' Mrs Holden frowned.

'Just a swab taken from the cervix, put on a slide— it's sent to the lab to be examined for abnormal cells. All women who are sexually active should have one taken regularly.'

'Well, that lets me out,' said Frances Holden with a grin. 'Chance would be a fine thing!'

Jenna and Daniel smiled.

'I think we should take one, nevertheless.' He glanced at Jenna. 'Nurse will tell you what that entails.'

The explanation was soon given and the smear taken. Frances dressed quickly and sat once more in front of Daniel. With the donning of her clothes she was once more the sophisticated woman she presented to the world.

'We'll let you know the results of the smear,' said Daniel. Jenna thought he looked pensive. He glanced through the patient's folder. 'How do you feel after the iron tablets?' he asked, glancing up.

Frances Holden looked guilty. 'Well. . . I didn't take them for long. They constipated me.'

'Well, try and take them. They'll help your tiredness. Eat plenty of fruit and vegetables as well.'

Mrs Holden rose. 'Thank you, Doctor.' She turned to Jenna. 'And you too, Nurse. You've both been very kind—kinder than I deserve.' She blushed.

Jenna went with her to the door.

'You know,' she said quietly, 'there are plenty of men out there ready to snap up a good-looking woman like you—plenty who prefer maturity and understanding.'

Frances Holden put her hand on Jenna's arm. 'Thank you, Nurse.' Her smile was tremulous. 'Words like that from a beauty like you do more to raise a middle-aged woman's confidence than any smile from a man!'

Jenna grinned.

As the door closed behind the patient, Daniel said, 'What magic spell did you use?' He was smiling.

'I just waved my wand,' she laughed.

'Perhaps you'd lend it to me. The change in Mrs Holden was fantastic.'

'You're too modest.' Her grin widened. 'Anyway, I

must go. No time to chat to doctors, no matter how good-looking they are.'

Daniel made to throw Mrs Holden's notes at her.

'Grrr!' he growled, as she opened the door with a laugh.

Chaperoning Daniel meant that Jenna had to leave two of her dressings until the afternoon. This made her late returning to the Health Centre, so it was half-past five before she had finished her paperwork.

All afternoon she had wondered about Daniel's casual reference to his fiancée being in America. Did this mean that his feelings towards Elaine had changed? Did it mean his interest in herself was greater than she had supposed? Jenna decided that this was her opportunity. If she wanted him, now was the time to go for him. And she did want him—oh, how she wanted him, but not just in bed. She wanted a life companion.

How could she have thought her love for him had died? His dinner invitation must mean something. He had said that there was no need to tell his fiancée, so. . .

Jenna had no compunction about taking him from Elaine. She had a feeling that Elaine thought of herself first. Jenna thought she had more to offer, and wasn't Daniel attracted to her? And weren't they on an amicable footing?

Having convinced herself, she hummed as she drove home. Hungry as she was, she decided that her choice of dress for the evening was more important.

I hope he's a good cook, she muttered to herself as she opened the wardrobe door.

Her more subdued clothes beckoned, but she was excited, and reached for a red two-piece glowing from the back. It seemed to reflect her feelings.

She arived at sixty-five, Stanley Road at exactly seven-thirty. The house had two storeys with bay windows on either side of the front door. Ivy covered the walls, so the effect was more like a leafy bower with a roof on top. There was a garage attached. A garden, divided by a path, was set out in formal lines, with borders of perennials. As she rang the bell, Jenna wondered if Daniel was the gardener.

He answered it and led her through the parquet hall into the lounge. It was decorated in pale greens, cool and refreshing, and Jenna looked like an exotic flower in its midst. It was the perfect setting for Elaine, she thought, and wondered if the décor was of her choosing.

Daniel was watching her. 'Like it? Elaine chose the colours.'

'Yes, very much.' Had she been wrong in thinking Daniel's offhand reference to his fiancée meant his relationship with Elaine was cooling?

'I'd offer you a sherry, but you're driving. . .'

'That's all right,' she assured him.

The cool room seemed to have affected them. Their words sounded stilted.

'Dinner's ready,' he said, gesturing for her to precede him. 'I'll show you over the house after we've eaten.' An amused smile hovered about his lips.

Jenna smiled back. She must have imagined his coolness.

The dining-room had mahogany furniture and magnolia-painted walls. It was a solid dependable room, like its owner.

'I hope you like prawns,' said Daniel as he seated her at a table large enough to accommodate ten.

'I love prawns.'

The meal was delicious. Fillet steak, perfectly cooked, followed the prawn cocktail. Black Forest Gâteau that melted in the mouth was a sweet Jenna resolved to try making herself. The cheeseboard had a selection of her favourite cheeses and was followed by a tart coffee she enjoyed. The conversation was mainly about books and films, their tastes similar yet divergent enough to stimulate a friendly argument.

As Jenna sipped her coffee, she said, 'You can come and cook for me any time.'

'I'm afraid I can't take the credit,' Daniel smiled. 'There's a little lady in the kitchen who cooks for me, and the gâteau was made by Elaine.'

'She's an excellent cook,' Jenna said, glad she had eaten the gâteau before he told her, knowing it would have choked her otherwise.

'Yes, she's a very accomplished lady.' Daniel's eyes were on Jenna's dress. It was an absentminded look, but she presumed he was implying that her bright dress showed lack of taste and that she was not in Elaine's class.

'Looks can be deceiving,' she said, meaning herself.

'Why don't you like Elaine?' he asked, frowning.

His words took her by surprise, so that she answered without thinking, 'Are you sure she's the right one for you?'

'Yes.' His eyes became cold. 'Why? Did you think you were?'

Her thoughts were out in the open. It was as if he had plucked them from her mind, and she could not stop herself.

'More suited to you? Yes.' Her passionate nature spat the words out. She could not hide her longing for him.

'I could never marry you, Jenna.' His words were quietly spoken, and they tore at her heart. 'It would never work. There's something disruptive about you that causes chaos, and I like peace.' He sighed deeply, almost regretfully, but she did not see that. 'Oh, I'm sure we'd have a great time in bed, but that's not enough.' It was the red dress that was making him talk like that, he told himself. Its colour signified passion—danger, and Jenna was both those things—passionate, dangerous.

At one time he had thought he had seen a different side to her, that night he had had risotto in her flat, but tonight, as she sat there glowing against the mahogany background—vibrant, alive—he longed for Elaine's coolness. Yes, there lay his destiny, his peace.

'I'm sorry if——' he began.

'There's no need,' Jenna interrupted him before he could say more. She was humiliated enough. 'I wasn't speaking of love; I was thinking more of passion.' She could not bear him to think she was in love with him, and was proud at how steady her voice was. Her features were composed, her brown eyes unreadable. Had he imagined the longing he had seen there?

She rose. 'It's time I was going.' Her tone was even, untroubled.

Daniel escorted her to the front door. 'Goodbye, Jenna,' he said, his expression tight, his body stiff.

Jenna nodded, unable to speak. It was taking all her courage to maintain her dignity.

As the door closed behind her, it closed on her hopes. She remembered saying to someone who had professed love for her, 'You can't expect someone to love you because you love them.' Never had she thought the words would apply to herself.

CHAPTER EIGHT

OVER the next few days, Jenna's optimistic nature reasserted itself. So she was in the position so many of her admirers had been in; so now she knew how they felt. She did not like it, not one bit, but she was not going to sink under it. She was going to fight. She realised, when she had recovered from her embarrassment and distress, that Daniel's invitation to dinner was to repay her for chaperoning him with Frances Holden, just as he had said. It had been her own longing that had read more into it.

But Elaine—what of her? Did she love Daniel? Perhaps, but Jenna suspected it was a love of convenience. After all, Elaine must be in her early thirties. There weren't many men of her age-group left unmarried.

Well, Elaine was not here now. Perhaps if Jenna tried to be more like the cool beauty, Daniel would see her differently. Some hope a small voice cried inside, but Jenna ignored it.

Richard's presence at coffee-time was not a strain any more. He was almost a different man. A couple of days after his return from holiday at the beginning of October, Jenna and he were alone in the staff-room. Penny was late and Daniel was held up with a patient.

'I'd like to thank you, Jenna,' he said, looking at her with eyes so like Daniel's that she could have wept, 'for being so kind to Susan. I'd also like to apologise for my behaviour that night.' His eyes were full of pain. 'I'd no right to treat you so. . .' He paused to think of a suitable word, then said, 'cavalierly.' His face had that serious expression that Daniel's had when *he* looked thoughtfully at her. 'I can't think of anything to say that will excuse me. I only hope you can forgive me in time.'

'Don't worry about it. I've already forgotten,' Jenna smiled.

'But I never will.' His voice was sincere. 'If there's ever anything I can do for you. . .'

Daniel came in at that moment, and Richard did not continue.

'I have to go.' He rose to his feet.

As the door closed behind his brother, Daniel said, 'I'm glad I caught you. Frances Holden's smear report is back, and it shows some abnormal cells. I've made an appointment for her to see me tomorrow.'

'Did you tell her the result?' she asked.

'No, not over the phone. I did tell her it wasn't anything for her to worry about.' He sighed. 'As you know, abnormal cells don't mean that she has cancer of the cervix. Could you be there when I tell her? It would give her moral support.'

How thoughtful he was! Jenna smiled. She had a busy schedule next day, but what did that matter? Daniel and Frances Holden needed her.

'I'll be there,' she said. Suddenly she remembered how there had been something familiar about Frances, and she knew what it was. They were alike in their attractiveness to men. Will I be like Frances Holden one day? she wondered. Always searching for another man as right for her as Daniel? Had Frances suffered from unrequited love?

Jenna was so busy with her own thoughts that she only caught the end of what Daniel was saying. '. . .smear test?' in an enquiring tone. She thought he was asking about another patient and said,

'Smear test? For whom?'

'For you.' There was impatience in his voice.

Jenna blushed. She wasn't going to tell him she was a virgin, and she wasn't going to tell a lie, so after a pause, during which he was looking at her with a thoughtful expression, she pretended to be offended, and said, 'That's none of your business!'

'Of course it is,' he said roughly. 'It's my duty to ensure that all the women in my care are encouraged to have this test.'

All the women in my care—— If only I were really in his care, she thought with longing, and turned away to pick up her bag so that he would not see the pain in her eyes.

'I'll bear it in mind,' she said. 'What time do you want me tomorrow?'

'Eleven o'clock, same as last time. You are registered with a doctor, I suppose?' Daniel asked, pouring himself some coffee.

Jenna had the door open. She wasn't registered. She had meant to, but it kept slipping her mind. Turning to face him, she said, 'No. Who would you recommend?'

A wry smile crossed his face. 'Dr Raymond. She's a very good female doctor.'

Jenna smiled. 'Is she a feminist?' she teased.

He nodded, his eyes twinkling. 'Probably. She has six sons—enough to make any woman a feminist, I should think, if only out of self-defence!'

He laughed, and Jenna laughed with him. 'She sounds just the doctor for me.'

Daniel's face straightened. 'Right. Register with her, then.'

Jenna snapped to attention. 'Aye, aye, sir,' she said, and left him grinning.

Next day, she organised her work so that she would be free for Mrs Holden's appointment. She was in the staff lounge pouring coffee when Daniel came in.

He smiled. 'Good—you managed to make it.'

Jenna was looking particularly attractive this morning. Her hair had been cut short, close to her face, and it drew attention to her cheekbones and the lines of her mouth. It drew more than that. It drew from him an admission that his attraction for this girl went deeper than he was willing to acknowledge. Daniel touched his breast pocket. A photograph of Elaine lay close to his heart. Whenever he felt tempted, as he was now, Elaine's presence, even though only on paper, steadied him.

He accepted a mug of coffee Jenna was holding out to him. 'One sugar, just as you like it,' she said, smiling.

'Thanks. You're looking after me very well.' His smile reflected hers.

Jenna deliberately brought his fiancée into the room by saying, 'We don't want you pining while Elaine's away.'

Daniel searched her face. Was she being sarcastic? But her face was bland, and he was so attuned to her——Attuned? No, that was the wrong word. So used to working with her—that was it. How could he possibly be attuned? he derided himself. So used to working with her, he repeated to himself, that he could tell if her expression was false. Couldn't he?

'If there's anything else I can do.' She spread her hands, her eyes laughing. She was teasing him.

'Only have a cervical smear,' he said drily, ignoring her banter. 'Romance doesn't come into our relationship, Jenna,' he said, his face serious. A desolation stole into his heart, making his eyes cold.

Damn! she thought. That backfired, but she wasn't going to be put off and said, giving him one of her most beguiling smiles, 'Pity, isn't it?' and laughed in a light-hearted way, her eyes mischievous.

'I never know how to take you, Jenna,' he said, his eyes bewildered.

'Just a regular Mona Lisa, me,' she smiled mysteriously.

Daniel laughed. He could not understand why he had taken her comment seriously.

Glancing at his watch, he said, 'Time we were going.'

It was almost as if the intervening days since Mrs Holden's last visit had not taken place. Everything was so much the same. Mrs Holden was wearing the same outfit, Daniel the same suit. Jenna, in uniform, was standing in the same place. Just their expressions were different. Daniel's was kind; Frances Holden's apprehensive, and Jenna's sympathetic.

'I have your report back,' said Daniel, holding it in his hand, an encouraging smile on his face.

Frances's bracelet jangled as she clasped her hands tightly together.

'Your report shows some abnormal cells.' Seeing her face tighten with anxiety, Daniel hastened to add, 'This doesn't mean to say that you have cancer of the cervix.' He gave a quick smile.

'What does it mean?' Frances's voice was a whisper.

'It means that you'll have to have another examination. It's called a colposcopy and involves an examination which will give you no more discomfort than having a smear taken.'

'A col—col?' Frances struggled with the word.

'A colposcopy. It's a sort of magnifying system that uses a bright light. The area from which the cells have been shed can be identified and a little piece will be taken. It gives you a slight pinching sensation, that's all, when it's removed. The little piece is sent to the lab for analysis.'

'Is that all?' Frances sounded relieved.

'Just about. When the results come back, you'll probably have further treatment to destroy the surface cells, using a laser.' He sounded very confident. 'I can assure you that the discomfort you'll feel will be minimal and the cervix will return to normal afterwards.'

'I have great confidence in you, Dr Daniel, and thank you for explaining it to me.' Frances said, smiling.

'I'll make an appointment for you to attend the

colposcopy clinic.' Daniel gave her one of his very special smiles.

She rose. 'Thanks for everything.' A broad smile chased the worry lines away. 'If I were a few years younger, Nurse,' she said, glancing at Jenna, 'I'd give you a run for your money! There aren't many men you'll find with good looks and kindness. Hold on to this one.'

I've got to catch him first, thought Jenna, but she said nothing.

When she had shown Frances Holden out, she turned back into the room. Daniel was writing up his patient's notes, his hair had fallen over his brow so that he looked like a little boy doing his homework.

'She's a great lady, is Frances,' said Daniel, closing the folder and looking up at Jenna.

'Yes. I admire her.' Jenna smiled. 'She'll be all right.'

'Yes.'

Somehow, their affection for Frances drew them together.

Daniel saw compassion for Frances still lingering in Jenna's eyes, her face soft with concern, and a picture of Elaine sprang into his mind. They had been out and Daniel had seen an elderly, worn lady trying to cross the road. He had hurried forward to assist her, but Elaine had remained where she was. When he rejoined her he was disturbed to see the hardness in her eyes. It was only there for a moment, and she had linked her arm in his, but he had felt compelled to ask, 'Don't you care for old people?' and her reply of, 'They must learn to look after themselves,' had concerned him further. When she had seen how her words had affected him, Elaine had softened her face and smiled. 'I didn't mean it quite like that. I'm very fond of my aunt.' And this explanation had satisfied him until now.

'I have to go,' said Jenna.

Daniel was glad to have his thoughts interrupted.

Sometimes Jenna had a way of making him look at things differently.

'I'll see you on Saturday at Susan's, in case I miss you tomorrow.'

Jenna paused halfway out of the doorway. 'Oh. Are you going to be there?' Susan had not told her when she had invited Jenna for dinner.

'Yes.' His eyes twinkled. 'She thinks I should get out more. Elaine was supposed to be home on Saturday, but her fashion house wants her to go to California, so she won't be home for three weeks.' Somehow, to his ears, it sounded as if it was an invitation for Jenna. . . He quickly corrected it with, 'I miss her.'

But did he miss her? He missed Jenna when she was late in for coffee. He missed seeing her car in the car park on her day off. He missed hearing her voice on the phone consulting him about a patient. . .

'I'll see you then if not before,' said Jenna. His reference to Elaine being away for a further three weeks had not affected Jenna this time, and her mind was still on his, 'I miss her', but she managed to give him a smile before she went out, closing the door quietly behind her.

Daniel picked up Frances Holden's notes and put them in the 'seen patients' pile. If it hadn't been for Frances he wouldn't be having these thoughts. Her insinuating that he and Jenna were a couple had. . . He rose abruptly, knocking over his chair. Lifting it, he set it on its feet with a bang and went to call the next patient.

Jenna was dressing for the dinner on Saturday evening. She was depressed. It was her weekend off, and it had rained all day. She had gone into Swansford by bus, as parking on Saturday was difficult, and had stood for what seemed like ages, waiting for the bus home. When she eventually arrived there, she found she had forgotten the coffee, which annoyed her further. Her nail polish smudged as she reapplied it. Her new shampoo had fluffed her hair out too much and she could not decide what to wear. Finally she chose a red skirt and teamed it with a patterned blouse that did not really match. The whole outfit signified how she felt.

All I need is for the car to be too damp to start, she thought, but it went first time, and this cheered her up a bit.

She arrived at eight-thirty. Hearing voices when Susan let her in, she thought Daniel must already be there.

Her friend was excited. 'Oh, Jenna!' Susan smiled broadly. 'I want you to meet someone.'

So it wasn't Daniel. Jenna's curiosity was roused. A tall dark-haired man, with rugged, outdoor features and brown eyes, was facing the door as they entered the lounge. He was talking to Richard, his hand in Amanda's. When he saw Jenna a look of appraisal crossed his face.

'Jenna, this is my brother, Robert Baxter. He's come home from Canada on leave.' Susan's face was alive with excitement. 'He didn't tell us he was coming—he wanted to give us a surprise.'

'So this is the tenant you wrote to me about.' Robert held out his free hand. 'You were right—she is beautiful.'

Amanda cried, 'Hello, Jenna!'

Jenna greeted the child as she took Robert's hand, then looked up into his face. She immediately liked him. His expression was interested and friendly, not lascivious, as so often happened when she was introduced to a man. He was older than Susan, about Daniel's age.

'Isn't it super he's home?' Amanda jumped up and down with excitement. 'Uncle Robert brought me a musical box!' She caught Jenna's hand and pulled her. 'I'll show it to you.'

'In a moment, darling,' Susan smiled. 'Your uncle hasn't had a chance to speak to Jenna yet.'

'That's all right,' Robert said. 'I'll come too.' He smiled. 'May I call you Jenna?' And at her nod, said, 'Good.'

Richard had his arm round Susan. 'Daniel's late,' Jenna heard him say as she left the room with Richard.

Amanda's room was light and airy, and Jenna marvelled at how the child unerringly led her there.

Lifting a musical box, Amanda ran her fingers lovingly over the carved flowers on the lid before she opened it. A well-known lullaby filled the room with its tinkling, delicate sound. Amanda's face was ecstatic with joy.

Jenna knelt beside her. 'That's lovely, darling.'

'Now, young lady,' Susan's voice came from the door, 'time for bed.'

'Oh, must I?' Amanda pleaded.

'Yes, you must.' Susan's tone was firm. Then relented. 'But you can listen to your musical box.' She came over and gave her daughter a hug.

Amanda carefully put her box down on her bedside table and stretched out her arms. 'Thank you, Uncle Robert. Thank you very, very much!'

Robert lifted the slender child in his arms. 'It's a pleasure, sweetheart.' For a big man, he was very gentle.

He looked at Jenna over Amanda's shoulder and smiled. It was an easy, friendly smile, it said, I like you, and Jenna smiled back.

'You two go down,' said Susan. 'I think I heard the bell. Daniel must have arrived.'

Robert kissed Amanda and set her down. He held the door for Jenna to precede him. Daniel greeted Robert as they went into he lounge.

'Hello.' His hand was outstretched. 'It's good to see you again, Robert.'

Robert seemed to be generally well liked, and Jenna

was not surprised. This man was one of those people who was popular with both sexes.

Richard offered drinks, but both Jenna and Daniel refused; she was driving, and he was both driving and on call.

Susan returned. 'We might as well go in,' she said, smiling.

A large bowl of roses collected from those still flowering filled the air with their scent. The silver gleamed and the cut-glass wine glasses shone with rainbow colours. Pink tablemats complemented the roses. The tableware was reflected in the polished mahogany like the ghosts of past dinners.

Jenna shivered.

'Are you cold?' Robert asked, a kind expression on his face. 'Would you like my jacket?'

Jenna smiled. 'Thanks, but I'm all right. It was just someone walking over my grave.'

She was glad of his friendly presence. Robert drew her mind away from the love she had for Daniel. It was good to be able to relax and behave naturally.

He was good company. Seated opposite to him, she could almost forget Daniel sitting beside her. Robert amused them with anecdotes of his travels.

Later in the lounge, having their coffee, Jenna asked him, 'How long are you here for?'

'Six weeks.' His brown eyes were warm. 'It's not just a holiday. I've got meetings to attend in London.'

'Do you want me to move out?'

Jenna loved the flat and did not want to leave, and this must have shown in her face, for he said, 'Don't look so worried! I wouldn't dream of throwing you out. I'm too much of a gentleman,' and he grinned.

Jenna laughed. 'Well, in that case, why don't we share? There *are* two bedrooms.'

Robert did not even looked surprised. He was a

practical person, and this suggestion of Jenna's sounded good. 'Only if we halve the chores!'

'Done.' Jenna stretched out her hand and he took it in both of his. Hers was cold, his were warm. Releasing them, he raised his glass and said, 'Here's to a beautiful friendship.'

Something made her glance at Daniel, and she was surprised to see his look of disapproval.

'We're out of the Dark Ages now, Daniel,' she said tartly. 'Men and women do share flats together.'

'I was just thinking of your reputation, Jenna, that's all,' he said, his face stiff.

His reply made her remarks seem fatuous, and she blushed.

'Jenna's reputation will be safe with me,' Robert said, giving Daniel a wry look.

Daniel frowned. 'I wasn't doubting you, Robert. I was thinking of how it might look to others.'

'Very commendable!' Robert's tone was dry. 'By the way, I haven't congratulated you on your engagement. I hope you'll introduce me to your fiancée soon.'

'Elaine's in America,' Daniel told him, aware that Robert was using the engagement to change the subject. 'She comes home in three weeks' time.'

'Good. Perhaps you'll both come to the flat for drinks. That is, if my flatmate approves.'

'Fine,' Jenna smiled. 'When do you want to move in?'

'Will tonight be too soon?'

It was his flat, so she said, 'No, that'll be fine.' But she could feel Daniel's disapproval and she was a little surprised at his concern.

'Will it be all right with you if we go quite soon?' asked Robert. It's been a long day.'

'Any time you like,' Jenna told him. 'Do you have a car?'

'No. Do you?' He was looking hopefully at her.

'It's only a Mini,' she said with a smile, looking at his large frame.

'We'll manage.' And he grinned broadly.

Again Jenna had that feeling that Daniel did not like this arrangement, and it annoyed her, but he helped load the car without a word.

She wondered if it would move; the back seat was packed tight with Robert's baggage, and he was more heavily built than Daniel

Seeing how crowded they were, Daniel said, 'Look, I'll take you.'

Robert had the window down to say goodbye. 'No, no,' he turned to Jenna, 'we'll manage, won't we?' He grinned mischievously.

Jenna laughed. 'Of course we will.'

They left a smiling Susan, with Richard's arm about her. Daniel was standing a little apart, scowling.

'Daniel seems very protective of you,' commented Robert as the car turned into the road.

'He's concerned about a lot of people.' Jenna sprang to Daniel's defence. She glanced sideways at Robert, and, seeing his wry look, said, 'There's nothing like that about our relationship. He's engaged to Elaine.'

There must have been a touch of longing in her voice, for he said, 'But you'd like it otherwise?'

Jenna should have been annoyed at his questioning her, but she wasn't. She felt he was her friend and she needed to tell someone, so she said, 'Yes,' so softly that he almost did not hear her.

'Well, I wouldn't give up hope if I were you. Our staying in the same flat seemed to disturb him more than it should have,' he grinned.

Hope flared for a moment, then Jenna remembered Daniel's words—I could never marry you—and it died. It so distresed her that she nearly ran through a red light. It was only Robert's, 'Hey' that saved her.

Once in the flat, Jenna offered to relinquish her room.

'No, of course not.' Robert struggled into the spare bedroom with his bag. 'This will do for me while I'm here.'

She smiled her thanks and helped bring some of his smaller bags up. As she propped his badminton racket against the wall, she said, 'Would you like a game some time?'

'Sure. We could make a foursome with Daniel and his lady—that is if they play.' A mischievous twinkle in his eyes made her laugh, and she laughed louder when he said, 'Make him jealous.'

'They do play, but it won't work.'

He raised an eyebrow. 'Want to bet?'

'You're incorrigible!' she sighed, but his confidence raised her spirits.

'You want to fight for your happiness, Jenna.' Robert's face straightened. 'I lost mine by being too sorry for myself. I wallowed in self-pity and missed the signs that the woman I loved, and who was engaged to someone else, really wanted me. I didn't discover it until she was married.'

His eyes held a pain Jenna wished she could alleviate, but she knew no word of hers would help. She had to try, though, so she said, 'If there's anything I can do. . .?'

He grinned. 'Don't tempt me!'

Jenna knew it was said in fun and smiled.

'I'm so glad you're here,' she said. Robert seemed to have taken the place of her parents. He was dependable and would not make demands on her.

And so it proved during the next three weeks. They were constantly in each other's company. Robert was an amusing and attentive companion. Determined to help Jenna catch Daniel for herself, he made sure Daniel was frequently with them.

Robert invited his sister and brother-in-law out to dinner and insisted they brought Daniel with them.

'He's part of the family,' he explained.

Jenna was there at the time, and he gave her a wink behind Susan's back. Jenna found it hard not to laugh.

He found other ways to throw them together by arranging to play squash with Daniel, then dropping out and phoning him to say, 'Jenna will take my place.

On one of these occasions Daniel had given her a suspicious look, but she had raised her hands and said, 'Not my doing—honestly!'

Sometimes there was more pain than pleasure in his company. He was inclined to be stiff, almost on guard, but at other times she had seen a softening of his expression when she had turned to him suddenly. Gradually, as the days followed days in her company, he could fight himself no longer, and he relaxed. After all, what had he to be afraid of?'

Three weeks after the arrival of Robert, Elaine came home, and Robert suggested Jenna invite Daniel and his fiancée to play badminton instead of coming to the flat for a drink. So on the Monday after Elaine's return Jenna hoped to catch Daniel at coffee-time, but he did not appear. She needed to see him about Mrs Ledson, the diabetic, for when Jenna had visited her that morning Mrs Ledson had complained of a sore toe. Jenna had looked at it and found the ingrowing nail had caused an infection.

'Have you seen the chiropodist lately?' asked Jenna, for the rest of Mrs Ledson's toenails were longer than they should be.

'You remember that time I was away for a few days?' Jenna nodded. 'Well, she must have come then, because I found a note from her through the letterbox.'

'And you didn't contact her?' It wasn't said accusingly.

'I forgot.' Mrs Ledson looked apologetic. 'I can't remember anything these days.'

'Never mind.' Jenna patted her arm. 'I'll ring her and explain.'

She cleaned the toe and put a dry dressing on it until she had spoken to Daniel.

As he wasn't having coffee, Jenna went to reception and asked where he was.

'In surgery,' Shirley told her.

Jenna waited until Daniel came out for his next patient.

'Can I see you for a moment?' asked Jenna.

'These people have been waiting,' he told her brusquely.

'Monday morning blues?' she smiled.

He did not respond, his face was grim. 'Facetiousness is not a quality I admire,' he said.

His tone and attitude distressed Jenna. Why was he so cold and forbidding? Surely he was not still bothered about her sharing Robert's flat?

'I want to see you about Mrs Ledson's toe,' she said, hiding her hurt behind a professional mask.'

I want to see you—I want to see you all the time, her heart cried, but the expression on her face remained unchanged.

'You'd better come to the surgery, then.' He sounded cross.

The next patient was already on her feet. Daniel crossed over to her and explained that he would only be a minute.

The surgery was filled with a cold light. Winter seemed to be fast approaching. It matched the bleakness of his expression and the misery in Jenna's heart.

'Mrs Ledson's toe is infected,' she said bluntly. She was eager to leave his hostile presence.

'Do you want me to visit?' His expression was still stiff.

Jenna's depression lifted a little at this sign of his trust in her judgement.

'Not at the moment. I'll see how the antibiotic works first.'

Daniel raised an eyebrow. His stiffness left him and he looked at her with amusement. 'Yes, Doctor,' he said.

Jenna flushed. 'Well, you are going to give her an antibiotic, aren't you?' His previous coldness made her speak sharply.

'Yes, of course. I was only teasing.' He picked up his prescription pad. 'Is she allergic to penicillin?'

Jenna was regretting her sharpnmess. 'No.' She tried a smile, but it was stiff.

Daniel wrote rapidly and handed it to her.

'Thanks.' She did not look at him.

'Would you ask Mrs Taylor to come in, please?' He sounded so weary that Jenna took a closer look at him. He was sitting behind the desk, his shoulders bent, his arms leaning acros the desk's top.

'Are you all right?' Jenna tried to hide her concern beneath a brisk tone.

He glanced up at her. 'Yes.' His expression lightened. 'Just Monday morning blues, as you said.' His smile lifted the weariness from his face.

'I can't stand facetious doctors,' she said, grinning.

'And I can't abide cheeky nurses,' he said, laughing.

Jenna was so pleased that his coldness towards her had gone that she nearly forgot Robert's invitation.

'Oh, by the way, Robert and I wondered if you and Elaine would like to make a foursome for badminton this week?' she said.

To Daniel it sounded as if Robert and Jenna were a couple, and, to hide his sudden anger at this, he bent his head, flipped open Mrs Taylor's notes and said, 'I'll ask her and let you know.'

His tone was so offhand that Jenna's happiness plummeted. She was about to leave when she thought, Blow this—I'm not going to let him play with my emotions like this, so she said, repeating the words he had used to her, 'I never know where I am with you, Daniel.' Her tone was hard, and he looked up in surprise. 'One moment you're nice and the next—nasty,' she added.

She turned to go again, but swung round with the door open. 'And you haven't returned my umbrella!' She glared at him, then left.

She was sure, as the door closed behind her, that she heard him laugh.

CHAPTER NINE

WHEN she reached home at five o'clock, Robert greeted her with, 'Daniel phoned—says he and Elaine can play on Wednesday evening. He'll book the court, if that's all right with you.' Robert smiled and raised his eyebrows. 'He particularly said that I must check with you first.'

Jenna laughed.

'If it wasn't, I was to phone him. He's invited us to his place afterwards—says he has to return something to you?' Robert's eyes were questioning.

Jenna blushed, but did not satisfy his curiosity.

'Wednesday will be fine for me,' she said.

'Right. Come and get your tea.'

It was fish and chips that he had cooked himself.

'You're a good cook,' Jenna told him, thankful that she did not have to prepare something. 'I think I'll marry you,' she jested.

'Oh, no, I'm not going to be caught like that. My wife's going to do the cooking.'

Their easy camaraderie lifted Jenna's spirits.

'There's a good film on at the Cannon,' Robert said as they washed the dishes together after their meal. 'Would you like to go?' And he told her the title.

'Yes, very much.' It was a long time since she had been to the cinema.

She enjoyed the film, a murder mystery. It was pleasant to have an escort, especially one with old-fashioned manners who opened the door for you and bought you a box of chocolates.

I could get used to this, Jenna thought wistfully, her mind on Daniel. He was another of those people whose little courtesies towards women brought appreciative smiles to their faces.

On Wednesday evening, Jenna and Robert were the first to arrive in the foyer of the sports centre where Daniel had suggested they meet.

Jenna was studying the notices on the club board when she heard a gasp from Robert, and looked round.

Daniel was coming through the doors with Elaine. They had their backs to the light, but Jenna knew it was Daniel by the way he walked, and recognised Elaine by the carriage of her head.

She glanced at Robert, and was shocked to see how pale he was. Before she could ask if he was all right, he said in a voice from which the breath had been sucked out,

'Elaine Graham!'

Daniel had reached them, but Elaine had stopped on hearing her name. She looked at Robert and she too turned pale.

'Robert Baxter.'

It was as if Jenna and Daniel were not there. Robert and Elaine moved towards each other, arms outstretched. Their hands met and held, their eyes searched each other's faces.

'I never thought,' she whispered.

'I never knew your married name. Never wanted to,' he added.

There was an identical expression on Daniel's and Jenna's faces. Both their mouths gaped. They stood side by side, their arms hanging by their sides. Daniel's sports bag had dropped to the floor. It was as if they were spectators.

Then Daniel recovered and said, 'I take it you two know each other?' His face was expressionless, and yet Jenna felt his anxiety.

He really does love her, she thought, then she acknowledged that she had known it all along, but had refused to admit it. All the hope she had nurtured fell away like the autumn leaves falling from the trees outside, and Jenna wished Elaine had returned when she should have done, for these last three weeks seeing Daniel socially had warmed her and increased her love for him.

He had seemed to enjoy her company so that she had felt sure he had felt something stronger for her than friendship and mutual attraction. But now, seeing his distress at the way Elaine was looking at Robert, seeing the tight lips and the clenched hands, Jenna knew she never really had a chance.

It looked to her as if Elaine and Robert had to force their eyes from each other to look at Daniel. Robert still held one of Elaine's hands as they turned.

'Yes,' they said in unison, and glanced at each other with a smile.

'I knew Elaine some years ago, before she was married,' Robert told them.

Jenna realised that Elaine must be the loved one Robert had told her about and she was happy for him, but concerned for Daniel who looked stricken.

'Married?' he echoed, in a shocked voice.

'Yes, Daniel,' Elaine said quietly. Jenna saw Robert's hand tighten on Elaine's. 'I'm divorced,' she said.

People passed on either side of them, with their rackets and bags, intent on their pursuits. They chattered happily, unaware of the dramatic situation between the two couples.

Jenna was as shocked as Daniel when she realised that he had not known of Elaine's previous marriage. A crazy hope flashed into Jenna's heart, a hope she knew was groundless, yet which she could not suppress. It filled her whole being like a light—it glowed within her. She longed to throw her arms around Daniel and cry, I'm here—my love is constant, and was grieved that she could not. Daniel would not want it anyway.

'We can't talk here,' he said in a tight voice. He picked up his bag. 'And talk we must.' He was looking at Elaine, his face bleak.

Jenna knew that look. Daniel could not abide deception.

'I'll cancel the game.' He glanced at Jenna. 'Unless you and Robert would like to play?'

His voice sounded normal, but Jenna had come to know what a private person Daniel was, a person who concealed his feelings. He was not volatile like herself.

'I'd like to go with Elaine,' said Robert, his arm about her shoulders.

'That won't be necessary.' Daniel's blue eyes were cold.

'I think it is,' Robert persisted firmly.

Controlled as Daniel was, Jenna cold see how difficult it was for him to maintain his composure, and she said,

'Don't you think Daniel and Elaine should be left on their own?'

'No, I don't.' It was the first time Robert had raised his voice to her. Then his face softened. 'Sorry.'

A general move was made towards the exit. Robert and Elaine went first, but Daniel and Jenna's way was impeded by a group of teenagers.

By the time they reached the car park, Robert was driving away with Elaine. Jenna did not know what to say; she was as stunned as Daniel.

His face was bleak, his eyes grim. 'Well, I can't leave you here,' he said, in a tight voice.

'I can get the bus.'

'No.' Jenna could have wept at the resignation in his tone. 'I'll drop you first.'

Daniel drove off as she was clicking her seatbelt into place. It was so unlike him, for he was always very punctilious about the wearing of seat-belts and having them fastened before driving away. It showed how disturbed he was.

The car was filled with a tense silence. Daniel was holding himself so tightly that his skin had paled, even his hair seemed to have lost some of its colour, and his knuckles were white as they gripped the wheel. His teeth were clenched so hard together that the muscles of his face stood out.

When they arrived at Jenna's flat, Robert's hired car was there. Daniel turned off the engine, but did not immediately make a move. He just sat, gripping the wheel. From being pale his face flushed, and Jenna knew he was trying to control himself.

She sat beside him and concentrated all her being on giving him strength. Surely the power of her love would support him?

Daniel gave a great sigh that was partly a groan, and Jenna felt the tension of unshed tears behind her eyes.

They left the car and went into the building. Jenna had that apprehensive feeling she always had before an exam. It was ridiculous really. It was none of her affair. But what happened to Daniel happened to her. She thought she heard Daniel mutter, 'He wants to be on his home ground,' but she wasn't sure; the whine of the lift made it difficult.

Robert must have been watching for them, for he was standing with the door open when they stepped out of the lift. They followed him into the lounge, where Elaine was sitting, a gin and tonic on the table beside her.

The tension in the room gave it an alien feel. The neutral walls appeared grey, the beige three-piece suite brown; even Elaine's white shorts and shirt had a grey tinge. Everything looked unclean.

Jenna hurried to light the fire. Immediately the glow swept away the bleakness. Turning on the table-lamps and drawing the curtains helped as well.

'I'll make some tea,' she said, eager to escape the uncomfortable silence.

She took as long as possible over this. When she returned to the lounge she expected to find a heated argument in progress; that was how it would have been with her, but the room was silent, except for Elaine's quiet weeping.

Daniel was standing looking out of the window. It was too dark to see the river. As if her arrival broke the silence, he said, 'Why didn't you tell me you were divorced, Elaine.' He turned slowly, like an old man; even the lines on his face appeared to have deepened. He seemed more interested in the reply to this question than in Elaine and Robert's previous relationship.

Robert was standing beside Elaine's chair, his hand on her shoulder. The couple seemed so right together, far more so than Daniel had with Elaine. There was a marked change in the auburn-haired woman. The brittle look had left her face. She had always been beautiful, but there had been an underlying hardness that had shown in her eyes. This also had gone. Elaine looked like a different person. Even her body had relaxed; it was no longer taut.

Elaine glanced up at Robert as if for support before answering. His smile gave her courage.

'I remember your sister telling me, early in our relationship. . .' She frowned. 'I can't quite remember how it came about—how you didn't approve of divorce. She said that you felt marriage shouldn't be undertaken unless there was a good chance of success and that the partners should be compatible enough to be able to solve any problems that might arise.' She gave a deprecating shrug. 'So I didn't tell you about my divorce.'

Daniel leaned back against the windowsill. 'And were you ever going to tell me?' He raised an eyebrow. 'I noticed you became engaged without divulging your secret.' He could not keep the sarcasm out of his voice.

'You were the one who sprang the engagement on me,

if you remember.' Elaine spoke up with spirit. 'I didn't
have time.'

Daniel did. His attraction for Jenna had made him
blurt it out. Elaine and he had discussed marriage, but
now he recalled how she had evaded giving him a
straight answer. He had thought it was because of her
career, but now he knew he was wrong.

'Your aunt. . .?' he began.

'I asked her not to mention it.' Elaine's face was tight
with strain.

The clatter of cups distracted Daniel. Jenna was
pouring tea, and the normality of it made him want to
shriek with hysterical laughter. A cup of tea! The British
way to face adversity, poured by a woman who looked
Italian.

Jenna handed Robert and Elaine their tea and was
bringing his across. He did not take it from her. Her
dark sultriness gripped him and he felt as if he was
being torn apart.

If she had not taken over from Muriel, he would not
have announced his engagement so precipitately, Elaine
would have told him about her divorce and he would
have. . . What would he have. . .?

Jenna was appalled at the venom of his expression.
His anguish was not of her making. Her hand trembled
and the cup she was holding clattered in the saucer, tea
spilling into it.

Daniel made no effort to take it, so she went back and
sat on the sofa, stricken to the depth of her being.

How she managed to keep her hand steady while
pouring her tea she would never know. Her mouth was
so dry that she gulped it down and poured another.

The clink of cups on saucers was the only sound in
the room. Daniel was struggling to control his anger at
Jenna. He looked at Robert.

'Where do you fit into all this?' he wanted to know.

'I knew Elaine before she was married. I was in love

with her.' He smiled down at Elaine. 'She was infatuated with another man. I knew she was very attracted to me, but I didn't fight for her.' He glanced at Elaine again, his expression apologetic. 'If I had, things might have been different.'

Elaine was gazing up at Robert. He had taken her hand and was bending over her.

'I knew soon after I was married,' Elaine said, her eyes smiling into Robert's, 'that I'd made a mistake and that it was you I was in love with.' It was spoken as if Daniel and Jenna were not in the room.

Daniel straightened. 'It seems I've been lucky, then.' He could not keep the bitterness from his voice.

Elaine pulled off her ring and held it out to him. The firelight caught the diamond and made it wink obscenely.

'Keep it. I don't want any reminders.' His voice was harsh, his face stiff.

They did not even look at him as he left the room. Jenna followed him to the front door, but he ignored her and went out, leaving her to close it behind him.

Sorrow for him mixed with anger against him. Jenna felt as exhausted as he must. She did not want to return to the lounge and went, instead, to her bedroom, grateful for the peace she found there. She undressed, slipped on her housecoat. As she passed through the hall on her way to the bathroom, she heard the murmur of voices from the lounge.

After a hot soak she felt better and, returning to her bedroom, sank into bed. A glance at the clock told her it was only half-past nine, but it felt as if it was midnight, she was so weary.

She turned out the light and lay back against the cool pillows, but sleep eluded her. Daniel was now free—but was he? And what chance had she? He hated her.

Her thoughts went round and round. She heard Robert leave with Elaine and glanced at the clock. It was midnight. Her tossing and turning meant that she had eventually to rise and make the bed. When she did sleep, it was heavily, and she did not hear Robert come in.

CHAPTER TEN

THE morning came, but Jenna overslept. It was Robert's banging on her door that roused her.

'It's quarter to eight—you'll be late for work!'

Jenna almost fell out of bed.

'Are you all right?' Robert's voice came through the door.

'Yes,' she called back.

She was washed and in her uniform by eight o'clock. Robert had tea and toast ready for her in the lounge. Normally she would have quipped, 'Doing your housewifery chores again?' but today everything had changed. She felt uncomfortable with him and avoided his eyes.

'Thanks,' she said, drinking the tea and eating the toast as quickly as possible, more eager to leave him than because she was late.

'I'm sorry if you were embarrassed last night,' Robert said.

Jenna looked at him. He appeared anything but sorry. The shadow of sadness that, she only realised now, had been part of him had gone. He looked younger, and she could not help but be pleased for him.

'I wasn't embarassed,' she smiled. 'I just felt in the way.' She put down her cup and it clinked on the saucer, reminding her of that other cup that her trembling hand had caused to rattle when Daniel had looked at her with hate. It was a moment before her composure was restored. 'I was just sorry for Daniel.' Her face straightened. 'It was unkind of you to bring Elaine here. It added to Daniel's pain.'

There was no regret in Robert's face as he said,

'I felt it would be easier for Elaine to face Daniel here rather than at his home.'

'You could have told him rather than let him see your car here.' She frowned in anger.

'Yes—well.' He shrugged. 'What's done's done.'

'What happens now, then?' She did not want to argue.

Robert followed her into the hall and helped her into her coat. 'Elaine and I are to be married as soon as possible, so she can come back with me to Canada,' he told her.

Jenna paused with the front door open. 'And her job?' She could not keep the astonishment out of her voice. Elaine's career had seemed to Jenna to come first.

'She's giving it up.'

This convinced Jenna that Elaine really loved Robert, and she said so.

'Yes,' he said simply. 'And I her.'

Jenna, while feeling pain for Daniel, could not help but smile. 'I wish you both every happiness,' she told him.

She was about to close the door after her when she felt it resist; Robert had caught hold of it.

'Now's your chance,' Jenna,' he said, smiling.

She looked at him with dark eyes full of sadness.

'If only that were true!' And she hurried away, close to tears.

When she arrived at the Health Centre, Daniel's car was not in its space. Was he all right? Jenna worried, as she made her way to the district nurses' room.

Penny was there before her and she looked up from her Kardex. 'You're not looking too happy today,' she commented.

Their relationship had improved since Robert had arrived and was living in the flat. Penny had greeted Jenna's fondness for him with hope. She still yearned for Daniel, and, if she could not have him, she did not want Jenna to.

'I didn't sleep too well,' Jenna said, putting her bag on the table with a thump.

'Robert keeping you awake?'

It was unlike Penny to be sly, and Jenna looked at her. Penny blushed. Jenna was tired and worried about Daniel, or she would never have let Penny's words goad her into saying,

'There's nothing between Robert and me—I've told you that before. Perhaps you'll believe me when I tell you he's going to marry Elaine.'

As soon as the words had left her lips she knew she should not have spoken. It was not her place to tell anyone about Daniel's broken engagement

Penny looked stunned. 'You're kidding me?' Her work list was forgotten.

Jenna did not reply, but her face showed she had been speaking the truth.

'Poor Daniel,' said Penny, but her eyes held speculation rather than compassion and Jenna knew what she was thinking.

Jenna collected her Kardex and sat down. Penny had more of a chance than she had to capture Daniel—the thought pained her.

'I hope you won't tell anybody about Daniel's broken engagement,' she asked anxiously.

Penny had risen and was looking out of the window.

'No, of course not,' she said. Then she added excitedly, 'Here's Daniel now.'

'I don't think he'll be quite ready for your comforting arms just yet,' Jenna said drily.

Penny turned, her eyes wide as she exclaimed, 'You're jealous!'

Jenna made no reply. Penny's delight was almost palpable as she took her seat and lifted her pen.

Jenna looked across at her. 'How's Charlie?' she asked.

It wasn't like her to hit back, but she felt so frustrated

where Daniel was concerned that she wanted to hit out at anything.

'Charlie's fine,' Penny said airily.

They were just about to leave and were standing, bags in hand, when there was a knock on the door, followed by Daniel.

'Ah, Jenna!' You would never have known his life had been shattered, for he looked just the same. 'I'm glad I caught you. I'd like to see Mrs Ledson's toe. Could we meet there?'

'Yes.' Jenna's expression was bland. 'I was going there now, though. Would you like to come with me?'

Daniel thought for a moment, then said, 'No, I'll follow you in my car.

He was about to leave, when Penny said, 'I was so sorry to hear about your broken engagement.' Her eyes were full of sympathy. 'If there's anything I can do. . .?' It was plain what she meant.

Jenna was appalled, but the hurt of having her confidence betrayed vanished when she saw Daniel's anger and heard him say to her, 'How dare you tell everyone about my private affairs?' His hands were clenched, his eyes furious. Jenna was quite sure that if she had been a man he would have punched her.

She could not deny it, nor could she explain, for she felt dreadful because she had told Penny herself. It was as if she had betrayed Daniel, and as a result she looked guilty.

'I won't tell anyone,' Penny hastened to say.

Daniel controlled his anger with difficulty, but Penny wasn't to blame, so he said. 'It's not your fault, Penny,' his tone softening. 'Some people can't help being disruptive.' The eyes he turned to Jenna were cold; their blueness had that icy tinge found in extreme weather. Jenna remembered how he had accused her of being disruptive before. It was not fair. It wasn't her fault he was attracted to her. It wasn't her fault Elaine had found Robert.

Her own anger flared. 'I wish you wouldn't make me the reason for your misfortune!' She had to fight hard not to shriek the words at him. 'I'm not!' And she added rashly, 'I can't help it if you won't admit the truth.'

Daniel was livid. 'And just what is the truth?' he demanded.

Jenna could not stop herself now. 'That deep down you're relieved. That you loved Elaine, but weren't *in* love with her. That you've been saved making the mistake she did.' She was breathing so hard that she had to pause for a moment, then she added, 'That you deceived yourself.'

Daniel's pale face flushed with fury. He had always prided himself on being a realist, but this was too much.

'You have no right to speak to a senior doctor like that!' The fight to control himself was almost visible. His face was grim as he said, 'I suggest you tender your resignation. There's no way we can work together now.' Turning, his back stiff with fury, he stormed away, banging the door after him.

Jenna was horrified, not only at what he had said, but at her own words. Whatever had possessed her? Why couldn't she be controlled like he was?

She put her bag back on the table less gently so that the contents rattled, and, sitting down, put her head in her hands. She could not believe she had been sacked, or what amounted to it. Daniel was not empowered to do that. She was employed by Swansford Health Board, but she knew his recommendation for her dismissal would be accepted and she would *be* dismissed. No, she would rather resign.

'Gosh!' 'Gosh' was one of Penny's favourite expletives. 'What are you going to do?'

Jenna looked up at her friend and felt like crying, I don't know, but she stood up, lifted her bag and said,

'Do? Go to work,' in as matter-of-fact a voice as she could muster. 'The patients still have to be looked after.'

'But what about Mrs Ledson's toe?' Penny had to hurry to keep up with Jenna's quick walk. 'I'll dress it for you if you like.' It would be her chance to comfort Daniel. Hadn't his eyes softened when they had looked at her?

'No, thanks.' Jenna's tone was distant, as they passed through the main door. 'I'll do it,' she said, and she hurried to her car.

But in the driving seat she had to wait until she could control the tears blurring her eyes. And then the trembling started. It was just reaction, she knew. Gripping the steering-wheel, she waited until it had stopped.

She glanced at her watch before turning on the engine. It was past nine o'clock. She was late for Mrs Ledson.

It was a clear late October day, but the skies were blue and the sun shone. You could almost imagine it was summer except for the nip in the air. It should have been dark with rain. Such a day would have matched her mood so much better.

It did not help to find Daniel's car outside Mrs Ledson's house when Jenna arrived. She was sure he would have arranged to see Mrs Ledson another time.

Jenna was about to ring the bell when the door opened and Daniel stood there, bag in hand.

'I've given Mrs Ledson her insulin and looked at her toe.' His face was tight, his eyes grim. 'I've left the dressing for you to do. It's coming along nicely, but I've left another prescription for a further course of antibiotics.'

Treating Mrs Ledson had calmed Daniel. He had slept badly after the shock of yesterday, and Jenna's words had winded him. He could not, would not admit the truth of what she had said, for it struck at the foundation of his life.

If it had not been for the expression on his face Jenna

could almost believe the scene at the Health Centre had
not taken place, for his words and tone of voice were so
normal. But it had taken place, and Jenna was still
smarting.

'Thank you.' Her face was so stiff that she could
hardly move her lips. She stood aside to let him pass.
'I'll hand in my resignation as soon as I've got time to
write it.'

'Good.' It was short and sharp and therefore more
effective.

Jenna bit her lip as she went down the hall. 'It's the
nurse, Mrs Ledson,' she said in as firm a voice as she
could manage.

When she returned to the Health Centre at eleven-
fifteen, Daniel was not there, but Richard was.

'What's this Penny's been telling me about your
resigning?' he wanted to know.

'It's true,' she admitted.

'Why?'

Jenna could say, Ask your brother, but she did not
want to, and she was thinking rapidly for a suitable
reply when Daniel came in.

'Have you heard this nonsense about Jenna resigning?' Richard's eyes were wide with surprise as they
looked up at his brother.

Daniel wearily dropped his visiting book and case-
notes on to the table. 'I know,' he said, not looking at
Jenna. 'I asked her to.'

'You what?' Richard's mouth gaped. 'I thought you
two were a team?'

'Well, we're not any more.' Daniel spoke through
clenched teeth. 'Leave it, Richard, can't you?'

Richard stood up. 'No, I can't. I owe Jenna a lot. If
you don't want her, I do. You can have Penny.'

'I don't want Jenna. . .' Daniel's face was white with
anger '. . . in my life.'

Jenna could have wept. Daniel did not want her—he hated her, and Penny was only too eager to have him.

Richard ignored his brother's outburst. 'Good, then that's settled. We'll do a swap; you can have Penny.' Then, realising how it must sound to Jenna, he turned to her and said, 'If that's all right with you, Jenna?' His tone was very gentle. 'Would the change-over create any difficulties?'

'No. We relieve each other quite a lot, so we have a working knowledge of each other's patients.' Her voice was expressionless, her eyes bleak. She was standing beside the coffee machine, and Richard came over to her.

'I don't know what your differences are, but do stay.' His eyes were pleading. 'Susan and I value your friendship too much to see you go.'

How could she refuse? Susan was very dear to her, and so was Richard now. She had spent many happy hours at their house, more so since Robert had come.

'All right.' She attempted to smile, but her lips trembled. 'I'll give it a try, but I don't promise to stay.'

'That's all I ask.' He smiled and touched her arm.

'Richard, I'd like to speak to you alone,' Daniel said, his eyes as bleak as Jenna's.

Glancing at Jenna's coffee, Richard said.

'You'd better come to my surgery, then.' His voice was sharp. Ever since Jenna had helped Susan and, indirectly, himself, she was perfect in his eyes. He looked on her as the angel who had brought Susan and himself together. His face softened as he said to her, 'Ask Penny to wait for me if you see her. I'll leave word with Shirley as well.'

Jenna nodded. She thought, with the exit of the two men, that the tension in the room would go with them, but it was still there, like an immovable force.

Having drunk her coffee, she washed the mug and put it away, wondering how she could perform such mundane acts when her mind and body were in such turmoil.

I won't think about it now, she thought, and with a great effort succeeded. Concentrating on her work helped. Her first visit after coffee-time was to the Smiths. Vera's plaster was now off, but her wrist remained weak. Jenna's relationship with them had improved over the weeks. Her meticulous professional behaviour had allayed Vera's suspicions.

One day, when Vera had been called to the phone, about a fortnight after Jenna had started to look after him, Michael Smith had said, 'Don't pay any attention to the wife, Nurse. She has this obsession—she thinks every woman wants to go to bed with me.' He raised his eyes to heaven. 'If only they did!' It was said in a jesting manner, and he had laughed. 'It's her way of coping with her jealousy.'

'Thanks for explaining,' Jenna had said. 'It makes it easier to understand.'

Today Mr Smith was already washed and up when Jenna arrived. 'See?' he beamed. 'No need for your services any more, Nurse. I managed with just a little help from Vera.'

His wife smiled indulgently. 'I thought it would be a surprise for you. Would you like a cup of coffee, Nurse?'

She seemed eager to please, so Jenna accepted.

'Come into the kitchen while I make it, would you?' Vera's eyes were pleading.

'Sure.' Jenna followed her.

'No talking about me behind my back, now,' Michael joked.

In the kitchen, Vera made no attempt to make the coffee. She turned to Jenna. The kitchen light showed the deep, frustrated lines on her face.

'I'm sorry for the way I've behaved, Nurse. It's this jealousy. I find it difficult to cope with.'

'I'm sure you have no need to worry where your

husband is concerned,' Jenna said gently. 'He loves you.'

'I know he does, but I don't seem to be able to help myself.'

Jenna smiled. 'Why don't you make an appointment to see Dr Daniel? I'm sure he could suggest someone who could help you.' It was surprising how she could say Daniel's name in her role as a nurse without it tearing her apart.

'Do you think he could help?' Hope sprang into Vera's eyes. 'It would make such a difference to my life.' Unshed tears made her eyes seem larger. 'I don't know why Michael stays with me.'

'Because I love you.' Michael had manoeuvred his wheelchair to the kitchen door, his face gentle with love.

The tears fell from Vera's eyes. She reached for a piece of paper towel and wiped her face.

'So? Where's the coffee?' Michael's voice was bright.

Jenna smiled and reached for the kettle.

'No, Nurse.' Vera blew her nose and took the kettle from her. 'You sit down and have a rest.'

Jenna left shortly afterwards. It was surprising how therapeutic work could be. It helped to put things into perspective. She was even feeling better by the time she returned to the Health Centre at twelve-forty, pleased because she had managed to fit in a dressing which she had thought she would have to leave until the afternoon. But as soon as she saw Daniel's car her misery flooded back. Penny's was parked beside it. She was sitting at the table when Jenna came into their room, and Jenna had the impression that the other girl had waited for her.

'You've seen Richard,' said Jenna. There was no mistaking the triumph in Penny's eyes.

'Yes.' Penny tried to make her expression sympathetic, but she was too excited. 'Of course I'm sorry for you, Jenna, but at least you won't have to resign.' Even to her ears it sounded false, and she blushed. 'Look how bad that would have been on your CV. Your next employer would be bound to question it.' Penny knew she was talking too much, but Jenna's sombre expression was making her feel uncomfortable. 'The good thing, though, is that you know most of the patients.' And here her expression was genuine. When Jenna still did not speak, Penny's discomfort increased and she said, 'Richard suggested we change doctors after your weekend off, on Monday.'

That would mean she would only have tomorrow, Friday, to be Daniel's nurse. The thought saddened Jenna.

'I really am sorry, Jen,' said Penny, meaning it this time.

'Thanks.' It was said with a wintry smile. 'I'll survive.' After all, she could not blame Penny for betraying her confidence. She might have done the same to catch Daniel.

Impulsively, Penny said, 'Look, why don't you come and stay the weekend with me? It would be like old times.'

No, it wouldn't, thought Jenna, and was going to refuse, but she suddenly thought that Robert might like the flat to himself so that he could be alone with Elaine so she accepted.

On Friday, Robert was out when Jenna arrived home at six o'clock. Taking over from Penny had taken longer than she had thought. A note propped on the coffee-table told her that Robert would not be in until late. It was a relief to have the flat to herself.

She spent the evening watching television—anything to stop her from thinking. She went to bed early and fell asleep with her book still in her hand and the light on. Robert's coming in woke her.

As she turned off the light, the book fell on the floor, but she left it and went back to sleep.

CHAPTER ELEVEN

ROBERT was still in bed when Jenna rose next morning. He was still there when she had had her breakfast, and she wondered if he was avoiding her.

Penny had given her the spare key, so she packed an overnight bag, left Robert a note saying she would be at Penny's for the weekend and went.

As soon as she entered Penny's flat she was glad she had moved out. The discordant décor aggravated her and she longed to return to Robert's, but felt she owed him something for allowing her to share his home.

She put her bag in the green room and went into the lounge. At least the view was harmonious and the weather was still fine. She could not have coped with a grey day.

She stood by the window for a long time, and gradually the river's movement calmed her troubled spirit. She decided to go for a walk. She caught a glimpse of herself in the wardrobe mirror as she collected her jacket. Dressed in black, without make-up, she appeared sallow. Her general appearance of weariness made her seem older than her twenty-six years.

Picking up her black anorak and shoulder-bag from the bed, she was in the hall when the key turned in the lock and Penny, in uniform, came in, followed by Charlie.

'Oh!' Guilt sharpened the fair girl's features. 'I didn't think you'd be here yet.'

'I'm just going,' Jenna said, but could not help wondering why Charlie was with Penny when she was on duty. Her puzzlement must have shown on her face, for Penny said,

'Er—I just happened to see Charlie out walking and thought we could grab a quick cup of coffee.'

Jenna suspected her friend was lying and wondered how many times Penny had brought Charlie to the flat when she was working. But it was none of her business, so she said, 'See you later.'

As Jenna walked along the river bank, absorbing the peace, she supposed she might have to leave Robert's flat. He would not want her there now, so she must make sure she saw him on Sunday evening to ask him.

There was no sign of Charlie and Penny when she returned; even the coffee-mugs had been washed and put away.

Thoughts of Daniel tormented her, and she decided to go to the cinema. At least there her mind would be occupied.

She chose a thriller. As the weather was fine the cinema was almost empty. Only the lonely and those wishing to distract themselves were there. The lights were down as she took her seat. Another person arrived after the film had started and sat in the row in front of hers.

The film was good, but it did not hold her. She kept being drawn to the man who had sat to the left in front of her. And then she knew why. It did not need the sudden lightening of the screen to show her it was Daniel.

Jenna shrank back in her seat and her first thought was to leave, but just to be near him in the cinema's semi-darkened intimacy filled her bleakness with warmth. She was glad of her dark clothing and hair. She would be almost invisible dressed as she was.

And yet he must have felt something, for he kept turning, moving restlessly in his seat. Eventually, fearful that he would see her, she rose carefully and slipped away, hoping that if she removed her disturbing presence he would be able to settle and escape into the film's fantasy. She only wished she had somewhere to escape to herself.

She returned to Robert's flat on Sunday evening. Robert was alone. He looked relaxed and happy, and Jenna envied him.

'You didn't need to go away,' he said, rising from his seat beside the fire.

'I know,' Jenna smiled. 'But I thought you might like some time alone with Elaine.'

'Thanks.'

The easiness between them was back. Having eaten very little over the weekend, she found she was hungry.

'Any food in the house?' she asked.

Robert grinned. 'Not much. I'll phone for a pizza if you like.'

Jenna nodded.

While they waited she asked what he was going to do about the flat.

He frowned. 'I'm not sure yet.' He paused to think. 'I'm due to go back in a couple of weeks, and Elaine's coming with me. We'll get married in Canada—it'll be easier all round.' His face was thoughtful as he said, 'We told Richard and Susan today, but Daniel had already mentioned that his engagement was off. Richard was a bit stiff, but Susan understood, and by the time we'd had lunch with them and discussed it all Richard had come round.' He grimaced. 'Susan was disappointed when we told them our plan to marry in Canada, but she could see it would be for the best.'

He was interrupted by the bell; the pizzas had arrived. They ate in companionable silence. Robert had produced a bottle of wine which went well with the meal.

'So what about the flat?' Jenna asked as she collected the plates.

'I'd like you to stay on for now.' Robert lifted the half-empty bottle and glasses. 'We won't be back for a while—probably at least a year.' He followed her into the kitchen. 'I'll let you know well in advance if we decide we want it for ourselves.'

Jenna was delighted. She had come to think of the flat as her home—the one stable thing in her uncertain life at the moment.

On Monday morning she returned to work with a feeling of strangeness. Since joining the Health Centre in July four months ago, she had come to rely on Daniel as a doctor and had been beginning to look on him as a friend. What would it be like working for Richard? She knew he was competent, but did he have Daniel's flair for diagnosis? He often had to consult his older brother.

Jenna missed her regular patients, especially Mrs Ledson and Mr Robinson, but Penny's patients accepted her with only an odd grumble now and again—! 'I liked the fair nurse,' or 'Changes, changes, always changes. You just get used to one nurse and another takes her place.'

Jenna found it easier to work with Richard. The underlying tension, always there with Daniel, was not there with his brother. She could laugh and joke with Richard, whereas with Daniel the attraction between them did not make for as free a relationship.

It was at coffee-time on Wednesday that they were having a good laugh when Daniel came in. It was the first time Jenna had seen him since his engagement was broken and his subsequent request for her resignation.

Silently he poured his coffee. There was something so lonely about him that Jenna's heart ached. He glanced in their direction and she was sure she saw a look of envy in his eyes, but it was gone in a moment.

He was stirring sugar into his mug when he said, 'I thought you might like to know that Frances Holden's reports are OK.'

'Thanks.' She didn't want to sound too eager. Daniel had spoken quite naturally. Perhaps they would be friends in time. She smiled, but he did not return it. A feeling of unease settled between them that Richard's mentioning an amusing incident with a patient failed to alleviate.

The door burst open and Penny came in. 'Oh, sorry,' she apologised, her hands full of bags and dressing packs. Daniel hurried forward to help her, his hands touching hers as he manoeuvred her bundles. Penny's eyes smiled into Daniel's as they juggled the packs.

'Wouldn't it be easier to make two trips?' he said, laughing as he caught a pack.

'I'll do that next time,' she grinned, her happiness at Daniel's nearness sweeping the tension from the room.

'When are you going to show me your outrageous flat, Penny?' he teased. 'Have you seen her flat, Richard?'

'No.' Richard's eyes twinkled. 'Is there a general invitation?'

'No.' Penny's reply was sharp. 'I told Daniel about my colour scheme and he said he'd like to see it.'

Our little Penny's quite clever in her own way, thought Jenna sourly. That was one way to get Daniel on his own.

Suddenly she felt like an outsider. Her three fair-haired colleagues appeared to have been cast from the same mould. Jenna felt dark, deep, different alongside them. They were the cool ones, with their blue eyes and sunshine hair—the daylight ones, while she was the brown-eyed, sultry, passionate one—the warm, night-time one. She did not know whether she envied them or not.

The three of them were laughing over something Penny had said, except for Jenna, who was lost in her own thoughts.

'Didn't you think it was funny, Jenna?' asked Penny.

Jenna had never heard such confidence in Penny's voice before.

'Sorry, I missed it,' she apologised.

'I was just telling Daniel and Richard. . .' even the

way Penny spoke the doctors' names was different. Before she had always been a bit in awe of them '. . .how I stepped into the broom cupboard at a new patient's flat, thinking it was the front door.' She was laughing so much that she could hardly tell the story,

It was infectious. They were all laughing when the door opened and the receptionist, Linda, came in.

'What's the joke?' she asked.

This sent them into further paroxysms. Even Daniel's face was still smiling when his eye caught Jenna's, but his quick look away told her that he had not forgiven her.

'Could I have a word with you, Penny?' said Jenna after Linda had left a case-note Daniel had requested.

Penny cast her a reproachful look. 'Now?' She smiled up at Daniel.

'Yes, please. It's about Mr Douglas.'

'Oh-h?' Penny frowned. 'What about him?' Her tone was defensive.

Jenna did not want to tell her in front of the doctors, so she said, 'Come along to our room.'

'You can tell me here.' Penny did not want Daniel's attention taken from her.

Jenna sighed. 'Very well. Was there a reason for visiting him once a week?'

'Yes.' Penny's defensiveness was more marked. 'I kept him on the books to check that his leg ulcer wasn't breaking down.'

'But he tells me it's been healed for two months.'

Penny blushed. 'We—ell. . .' she thought rapidly '. . .he could knock his leg again.'

'I suppose he could if he was senile, but he's a sprightly, active man of sixty-five and quite capable of letting us know if his ulcer deteriorates.'

'Oh, well, if you think he doesn't need a visit. . .' Penny was offhand.

'And Mrs Skinner?' Jenna persisted. She had found

one or two more patients who should have been discharged and hadn't been. No wonder Penny managed to finish early if so many of her patients were just check visits!

'I told you about her.' Penny was beginning to wish she had accepted Jenna's request to go to their room. She had seen the thoughtful expression on Daniel's face.

'You told me that she needed general nursing care daily, but when I arrived this morning she was already dressed and washed by her daughter, and the coffee-cups were out,' Jenna said. She understood, now, why Penny had looked a little uncomfortable at their hand-over.

'We—ell,' again Penny had to think rapidly, and said, 'her daughter needed her confidence boosting.' And she smiled triumphantly.

'She looked pretty boosted to me,' was Jenna's dry reply. 'When I suggested discharging her mother, her daughter was delighted. She told me how she'd asked you about that, but that you'd expressed doubts. To know that I considered her capable of caring for her mother delighted her.'

'I thought it was part of a district sister's duties to lend patients' relatives support,' said Daniel, giving Jenna a cool look.

She stared him straight in the eye. 'So it is, but it's also her duty to teach the relatives to look after their loved ones and help them to feel confident that they can do so, and to judge when that time comes.'

'Hmm,' was the only comment he made, and it did not help Jenna's confidence at all.

Penny's face glowed. She obviously thought Daniel agreed with her. 'It's my soft heart,' she said, looking up at him with a simpering expression.

It made Jenna sound unfeeling, and it annoyed her to see Daniel smile at her friend.

Richard had remained silent, but Jenna saw his look

of approval and was heartened, though she wished it
had been Daniel who had looked at her so.

The two doctors left and Jenna was about to follow
when Penny said, with a sullen expression on her face,

'Did you have to embarrass me in front of Daniel?'
Her fair skin was flushed.

'I did suggest we went along to our room,' said Jenna
quietly.

'You did it because you're jealous that Daniel prefers
me!'

Jenna thought for a moment. Was Penny right? Then
she frowned. No, it was purely a professional matter,
and that was what she told Penny, adding, 'There are a
few more cases like that which I didn't mention.'

'Well, it's your district now,' said Penny, affronted,
and lifted her bag. 'You can do what you want with it!'
and she left.

Robert was due to leave in the middle of November.
Jenna had seen little of him and she missed his com-
panionship. Penny had remained distant, and Susan had
been busy, having offered to help in a charity shop, so
Jenna was feeling lonely.

She only saw Daniel at coffee-time, and he hardly
spoke to her then. He had lost weight, but the haunted
look about his face had gone. Jenna presumed Penny
had something to do with this; she had seen them
together on a couple of occasions—coming out of a
cinema, and once at a restaurant.

Jenna was late-night shopping when she saw Penny
with Daniel. Turning quickly to avoid them seeing her,
she bumped into Charlie.

'It's all your fault!' he said angrily when they had
righted themselves. His tone was accusing.

Jenna's mouth gaped. 'What is?' she gasped.

'Penny ditched me for that doctor of yours.'

Part of Jenna's mind realised that Charlie must have

been following Penny. 'Mine?' she echoed, a puzzled frown on her face.

'Yes. That Dr Daniel. You were *his* nurse, weren't you?'

For one wild, ridiculous moment Jenna had thought Daniel had coupled himself with her, but Charlie's words showed her how wrong she was.

'Yes,' she said wearily.

'Everything was all right between Penny and me until you changed doctors. Now she won't have anything to do with me.' His tone was quite threatening.

Jenna refused to be intimidated. 'Well, that's not my fault. She was keen on him before we changed districts,' she spoke up boldly.

He took a step nearer to her. 'You're lying! Everything would have been all right if you hadn't come to Swansford.' His face was white with anger. 'I——'

They were blocking the aisle between the counters. 'Excuse me.' A shopper was trying to pass.

With a last look of hate, Charlie turned and left.

Jenna stood unmoving. Was she such a disturbing influence? Daniel had accused her of being so.

'Can I help you, madam?' a familiar voice asked from close by.

Jenna looked in its direction and met a pair of disapproving eyes. She recognised the asistant who had caught her twisting the tube of make-up the day Jenna had watched Daniel gaze so lovingly at Elaine.

'No, thank you,' Jenna said evenly.

Remembering the humour of that encounter lifted her misery a little, but did not alleviate the pain deep inside her.

But as she walked out of the shop she was determined to leave her doubts behind her. Her confidence returned. None of the circumstances which had occurred since her arrival were her fault. Robert would still have found Elaine. Penny would still have been infatuated with Daniel.

Jenna held her head high, her face composed. Passers-by looked at the dark, attractive girl, some trying to remember if she was a film star.

CHAPTER TWELVE

A FEW days later Susan phoned. 'I'm giving a small party for Robert and Elaine—just the family and close friends. Would you like to come?' She spoke hesitantly to Jenna.

Because Jenna had stopped feeling guilty and had looked everybody calmly in the eye, her unconscious dignity had lessened Penny's hostility and they had become quite friendly again. It made working together much easier.

Daniel's attitude had changed as well. He was no longer as forbidding. On the occasions when she had had to consult him on Richard's days off, Daniel had treated her with courtesy and had even smiled.

Robert sensed the change in her, and the tension between them vanished. He brought Elaine to the flat and Jenna had joined them for a meal on a couple of occasions. Elaine knew she had no need to be jealous of Jenna where Robert was concerned, unlike Daniel. There she had wondered and worried just what his feelings were for Jenna.

So Jenna answered Susan quite happily. 'I'd love to come.'

'Good.' There was a smile in Susan's voice. 'It's on Saturday at seven-thirty. Amanda's away for the week-end, staying with a friend.'

Jenna had wondered what to wear and went late-night shopping on the Thursday before the party. Returning to the flat with so many parcels, she was unable to put the key in the lock, and pressed the bell.

The door opened and her face, already flushed with

the excitement of shopping, became even redder. Daniel was standing framed in the doorway.

He smiled. 'Have you left anything in the shops?' he asked, catching two of her parels as they slipped.

'Just a few things for you,' she quipped.

'Yes.' His smile broadened. 'The men's department isn't quite your style!'

He reached forward and took another parcel from her. His nearness was disconcerting; she had not been this close to him since their kiss.

He stood aside to let her pass and followed her into the bedroom, putting his parcels on the bed. Jenna crossed the room to the window and drew the curtains. The presence in her bedroom was adding to her tension. She turned.

Daniel was looking about her room. It was fresh and bright, decorated in soft shades of pink, but not that sickly pink. The effect was warm but not cloying.

There was an uncertainty about Daniel's expression when he turned to look at her. Jenna knew him so well she could read his thoughts.

'Not quite what you expected.' It was not said as a question, and it was hard to keep the bitterness out of her voice. Why was he here?

Before he could reply, Robert's voice came from the lounge.

'Come and see what Daniel has given us!'

So that was why Daniel had come. Jenna admitted her disappointment. For a secret moment she had thought he had come to see her.

When she went into the lounge, Robert was holding a large cut-glass vase. It flashed rainbow colours as he turned it in his hands, catching the electric light.

'Oh, it's lovely!' Her spontaneous admiration drew a smile from Daniel.

'Yes, it is.' Elaine spoke from the couch. Her smile as

she looked at Daniel held more than pleasure at the gift; there was gratitude there as well.

'I'm glad you like it,' said Daniel. 'It's more of a peace-offering than an engagement present.'

Jenna searched his face for hidden pain, but saw none.

'It's kind of you to forgive me,' said Elaine, the humility in her voice genuine.

'There's nothing to forgive.' Jenna thought his voice was just a little too bland. 'Robert's the man for you.' His smile when it came was relaxed. 'We'd probably have made a go of it, but. . .' He shrugged. There was no bitterness in his voice.

He picked up his jacket; it was black, and when he put it on his shoulders looked broader. 'I'll see you both on Saturday, then.'

Elaine had risen and appeared to be about to accompany Robert to the door.

'I'll see Daniel out,' Jenna offered, and received a grateful look from Elaine, whose face was tight with strain.

Daniel paused at the front door. 'I owe you an apology too, Jenna,' he said, his face serious. 'It was unforgivable of me to ask for your resignation, and I'm glad Richard found a better solution.'

This was not what Jenna wanted to hear. She was glad, of course, and he was looking at her with a friendly expression on his face, but that was all it was—friendly

Jenna looked at him thoughtfully. 'You all better now?' The childish question left her lips before she could stop it, but she had to know.

'I will be, given time. It takes a while to adjust your life, and it can't be done like changing a suit.' He smiled ruefully. 'I'm not as tough as I look.'

It sounded so vulnerable that Jenna placed her hand impulsively on his arm. 'None of us is,' she said quietly.

'Are you sure, Jenna? You seem to be taking Robert's engagement with equanimity.'

She looked puzzled. 'Why shouldn't I be?'

It was his turn to look surprised. 'I thought you and he. . .' He spread his hands.

'It is possible to share a flat with a man and not become lovers.' Her tone was wry.

Daniel looked at her for a long moment. 'I find that hard to believe.' A glint of amusement crept into his yes. 'Sharing with you would be too much of a temptation!'

So that was the reason for his disapproval when she'd suggested that Robert and she share. It wasn't concern for her reputation. Did this mean Daniel had been jealous?

Suddenly Jenna was angry with him. She knew he desired her—it was there in his eyes now. She knew his longing for her was as great as her own, and yet he had made no move to reach out for her. Even now, when Elaine no longer stood between them. . .

'Someone with your iron control shouldn't have a problem; why don't you try it? I need a place to stay.' The lie fell easily from her lips. The challenge was too tempting. 'And you have that great big house. . .'

A thoughtful expression settled on Daniel's face. He knew she was lying. Susan had told him that Robert was leasing the flat to her for a year. His hatred of deception goaded him into accepting her challenge.

'Right. When would you like to move in?'

For a moment Jenna was nonplussed. She was so sure he would have refused. 'Aren't you afraid of what the patients will say? I'm only thinking of your reputation.' She could not resist saying it.

'I'm not, if you're not.' There was laughter in in his voice.

'When would you like me to come, then?' Jenna was quite enjoying herself.

'Would tomorrow be too soon?'

Touché, she thought, and lifted the gauntlet.

'It would have to be in the evening,' she told him.

'That's fine. I could give you a hand after surgery.'

'Thanks,' she said.

'Will six-thirty be all right?' Daniel's face was bland, but she felt he was laughing at her.

'Couldn't be better.' She hoped the uncertainty she was feeling did not sound in her voice.

After she had shut the door behind him he took a deep breath. Had she bitten off more than she could chew?

'You were a long time seeing Daniel out,' said Robert when she joined them in the lounge.

'I think I've done a foolish thing,' Jenna said with a grimace, and told them. 'He was so damn patronising!' she explained, by way of an excuse. 'He thinks he knows everything.' She grinned at Robert. 'He thought we were having an affair.'

Robert laughed. 'Well, I did think about it,' he said, then, seeing Elaine's face, he said quickly, 'But it was only for a moment.'

'Not much of a compliment to me,' said Jenna, laughing.

After Robert had returned from taking Elaine to her aunt's, he said, 'Are you sure you'll cope?' His expression was concerned. 'Does Daniel know you love him?'

'I don't think so.' Jenna certainly hoped not. 'He's made it plain that he's not in love with me.'

'I wonder.' Robert looked pensively at her. 'Elaine told me he wasn't in love with her. Oh, he loved her, but he wasn't *in* love with her, if you know what I mean.'

Robert had used the same words that Jenna had to Daniel.

'But that doesn't mean he's in love with me,' she sighed.

She looked so miserable that Robert took her in his arms. She could smell Elaine's perfume on his sweater. But they were the wrong arms, and a longing for Daniel's arms about her gripped her so stongly that she knew she should not have suggested moving in. It would be torture for her to be under the same roof with him.

But an underlying excitement carried her through the next day.

'See you at six-thirty,' Daniel said as he left her at coffee-time.

Penny's eyebrows rose. 'Six-thirty?' Suspicion clouded her brow.

'Yes.' Jenna prepared herself for Penny's objections. 'He's offered me a room in his house.' She blushed at the deception.

Penny mistook the blush and echoed, 'In his house?' Her face was envious and even more suspicious. 'Why?'

'Robert's getting married. The flat——'

Penny interrupting her with, 'Oh, I suppose he wants to sell it,' prevented Jenna from telling a direct lie, for which she was grateful.

She felt she was sinking deeper and deeper into deception. She had already phoned Susan that morning. 'Don't tell Daniel I'm keeping the flat on,' she had begged.

'But——'

Jenna had thought Susan was objecting to the deceit, and rushed in to say, 'It will only be for a short while.'

'But——'

Again Jenna had interrupted her. 'Sorry, must go or I'll be late for work.'

'You could have stayed with me until you found another place.' Penny's face was pinched with dislike as she added, 'Or are you trying to take Daniel away from me?'

Yes, thought Jenna, if he's yours, but said, 'I thought it better not to ask you.' How deeply she was becoming involved with deceit! She hadn't thought that at all. 'I've imposed enough.'

Penny's face was doubtful. She did not believe Jenna.

'It's only a room,' Jenna pointed out. 'I don't expect I'll see Daniel much, so you've no need to worry.'

'Haven't I?' Penny's eyes were distrustful.

This time Jenna could not lie, so she picked up her bag. 'I'd better be going,' she said, and left quickly.

She was half out of the door when Penny said, 'Would you do Mr Robinson for me?'

Jenna turned. 'Why?'

'Oh, go on, Jenna! I really am pushed for time.'

'All right.' Jenna had enough to do herself, but she would like to see Mr Robinson again.

When she arrived at his flat, he said, 'That other nurse isn't like you. She always leaves me till later in the morning. You always came early.'

Jenna just smiled, but made no comment. She was opening the front door to leave and was startled to find Daniel on the step. She had forgotten that it was his visiting day.

'I thought Penny would be here.' His surprise was equal to hers.

So he was interested in Penny! A feeling of insecurity swept Jenna's new assurance away. 'I—I——' she stuttered, then, taking a grip on herself, she said, 'She asked me to do Mr Robinson because she's busy.'

'Oh, and you're not.' It was not an accusation. It was spoken in a kind way.

This gentling towards her, coupled with the thought that Penny might catch Daniel on the rebound, raised Jenna's hopes, and she smiled.

It was this smile, more than the change he had noticed in her since his demand for her resignation, that broke the tension he had always felt in her presence. There

was no allurement in it. Its very naturalness caused the
desire, suppressed so often when in her company, to
flare in his eyes, in the step he took towards her, in his
hand reaching out. Jenna's breathing became faster.

'Is that you, Doctor?' Mrs Robinson's voice came
from the lounge.

Daniel gave a rueful grin. 'Are you coming back in?'
he asked.

Jenna swallowed. 'No. I'd better get on.' She smiled.
'Must be ready for half-past-six!'

At six-thirty her bags and possessions were stacked in
the hall. Robert was out. When a quarter-to-seven came
without Daniel arriving, Jenna thought he must have
changed his mind. She was about to move her luggage
back into the bedroom when the bell rang.

'Sorry for the delay.' It was Daniel. 'I had an emergency.' Jenna had forgotten he was on call. 'A child with
a high temperture—teething problems.'

It did not take long for them to move her luggage to
Daniel's car. 'You follow in the Mini,' he told her.

When she parked her small car beside his larger one,
it seemed to symbolise the differences between them—
her vulnerability, Daniel's strength; her volatile nature
compared to his control.

As they entered the hall a voice came from the back
of the house. 'Is that you, Dr Daniel?' For a moment
Jenna thought it was Mrs Robinson, but it was a tiny,
bustling woman, with short grey permed hair, who came
into the hall wiping her hands on a towel. She looked at
Jenna with suspicion.

'Is this her, then?' The lines on the elderly face were
deep with disapproval.

Daniel grinned. 'Yes.' He went forward and had to
bend slightly to put his arm around the short lady. 'This
is Edith Williams,' He smiled up at Jenna. 'My guardian
angel.'

Edith Williams's expression became even more disapproving, but she did not move away from the shelter of Daniel's arms.

'This good lady. . .' He looked down at Edith '. . .is my housekeeper. She's a wonderful cook.' Jenna remembered, now, Daniel's reference to 'a little lady in the back' when she had dined that evening. 'I don't know how she keeps this large house in such immaculate condition, but she does.'

This time Edith did look up at him with a smile.

It was a relief to Jenna to find another woman in the house. This forbidding presence would prevent any emotional escalation of the attraction between them.

She smiled and said, 'How do you do?'

'Hmm.' The reply was a grunt. 'I hope you're clean and tidy and do your own washing?' Edith's eyebrows drew together with a frown.

'Yes. Just let me know if there's anything else I can do to help,' said Jenna meekly.

'Hmm, we'll see.' Edith looked up at Daniel. 'Your dinner's ready.' She glanced across to Jenna. 'Yours too.'

Jenna had already eaten, but she certainly was not going to say so. 'Thanks.' Both she and Daniel spoke together and smiled, but Edith just scowled, and scurried away.

Daniel gestured to the stairs. 'I'll show you to your room.' He lifted her suitcase.

The room was at the back of the house overlooking a formal garden. It reflected Daniel's ordered personality.

'I hope you don't mind the double bed,' he said, lifting her case with ease and putting it on to the green and white striped duvet cover. Green was the predominant colour in the room, but, unlike Penny's bedroom, here the shade was muted. It was restful.

'It's lovely,' she said, meaning it.

'I'm glad you like it.' He sounded pleased. 'This used to be my room when we stayed here as boys.' She wished he had not told her, for now she would visualise the young Daniel here.

'We'd better go and eat before Edith comes up here after us!' He smiled. 'Don't let her bully you. It's all an act. She'd hate anyone to know how thrilled she is to have another person to look after.'

He ushered her before him into the dining-room and pulled out her chair. It made her feel cherished, and she smiled up at him.

The starter was grapefruit. 'I should have asked what your food preferences are,' said Daniel. 'Grapefruit is among my favourites.'

'I eat anything and everything,' she assured him with a grin.

'It certainly doesn't show,' he commented.

Jenna blushed as he glanced over her figure. She did not tell him her slimness was his fault, that he was the cause of her loss of appetite.

'I burn it off very quickly—work, you know,' she smiled.

Edith came in with the main course. 'I hope you like Lancashire hotpot,' she said. 'My mother taught me how to make it.' She placed well-filled plates before both of them.

Jenna was not a stew or casserole person, but the smell rising from the plate was so appetising that she said, 'I love it,' and glanced across at Daniel, who was giving her an old-fashioned look.

'Now see you eat it all up.' Edith spoke to Daniel as if he were a child. She glanced at Jenna. 'You're a nurse, so you make him. He's not been eating enough lately.'

Jenna managed to keep her face straight with difficulty. 'I'll do my best,' she promised.

'Hmm,' Edith grunted, and the plates rattled on the tray as she hurried from the room.

Daniel and Jenna both laughed. 'You must forgive her. She was with my grandfather, and when he died

and left the house to me, it was on the understanding
that Edie was kept on.' He poured her some wine.
'What about your family?'

'My parents are in Arizona.' And she explained about
her mother's asthma.

'So that was why you behaved as you did when you
first met Mr Robinson?'

'Yes. I couldn't help myself.'

'You should have told me,' he said sternly.

'You weren't very approachable, if you remember.'

Daniel did. Looking across at Jenna now, she seemed
a different person, or was it he who had changed?

'All that's behind us now,' he said.

Jenna studied his face. Was this an offer of friendship?
Could they ever be friends? Wasn't the attraction
between them too great? She could feel it in the silence
of the room. Tension—sexual tension, building, building as they ate.

'Miss Jenna.' Jenna's eyes had been concentrating on
Daniel so hard that she had not heard Edith come in.
'You certainly know how to handle Dr Daniel. That's
the first decent meal he's eaten for ages!'

Jenna smiled. She was delighted that she had gone up
in Edith's estimation. The empty plates were replaced
with a large portion of lemon meringue pie.

'I see I'll be putting on weight if you feed me like
this, Miss Williams,' Jenna smiled.

'Call me Edie.' The severe face relaxed into a smile.

When she had left the room Daniel laughed. 'You're
certainly in Edie's good books!' The tension had gone.

'Only if you finish every bit of your dinner,' Jenna
admonished with a severe expression which she spoilt
by laughing.

'You'll have to stay here and see that I do, instead of
looking for another flat.' His eyes narrowed.

'We'll have to see how we get on living under the
same roof first.' Why hadn't she told him then instead

of sinking deeper and deeper into this foolishness? She should admit it right now and return to Robert's flat. But a chance like this might never come again. If he saw her every day in a domestic setting he might. . .

Daniel smiled. 'What about a month's trial, and if it's a success you'll be here for Christmas. My parents are coming, and perhaps yours would like to as well.' He was pressuring her deliberately, hoping she would confess that she did not need a lodging.

'I think that's going a little too fast,' Jenna protested. 'I've only just arrived!'

A look of disappointment crossed his face. Jenna thought it was because of her reply, and hope rose in her heart—she ate her lemon meringue pie with gusto.

'Would you like coffee?' he asked, when she had finished.

He seemed to have distanced himself, and this puzzled Jenna.

'Yes, please,' she said, hiding her discomfort behind a smile.

He rose. 'You go into the lounge and I'll bring it.'

The curtains were drawn. Jenna poked the fire in the grate and added some coal. It was burning well by the time Daniel joined her.

'I ought to help Edie with the washing up,' she said.

'No need—we have a dishwasher.' He grinned. 'And it's not Edie!'

Jenna laughed. She loved it when he was relaxed and she was pleased his former distancing had been temporary.

Edie appeared a few moments later. 'I'm off to bed.' She looked at Jenna. 'I usually cook bacon and egg for the doctor's breakfast. Will you take the same?'

Jenna, who went to work on coffee and toast, said, 'Yes, please,' not daring to answer otherwise. She could see Daniel grinning out of the corner of her eye.

Edie nodded her approval and left them.

'I think the house would fall down if Edie weren't here,' laughed Daniel.

'Were you going to retire her when Elaine. . .?'

It wasn't like Jenna to be so thoughtless, it was her anxiety over Daniel's previous coolness, still with her, that had made her speak without thinking. 'Oh, I'm sorry,' she said, aghast.

'That's all right.' He sighed. 'There was a lot of truth in what you said. I wasn't in love with Elaine.' The words were spoken bluntly, and Jenna knew what it had cost his pride to admit she was right.

His eyes were intent, and she searched in them for some encouragement for herself, but found none.

They drank their coffee and discussed general topics. Daniel gestured towards the bookcase. 'Help yourself to any of these, if you like.'

'Thanks, I will,' she said, wondering if she would be in his house long enough to finish one. She was enjoying his company so much that she knew it would be impossible to leave if she stayed for any length of time.

Sleep eluded her that night. Her thoughts were with Daniel in the room opposite. Did he sleep on his right or his left side? Did he wear pyjamas? The thought of his muscular body lying between sheets like hers made her breath quicken.

She smiled as she remembered how they had crept upstairs, suppressing their giggles so as not to wake Edie. She had not known Daniel could be such fun.

A sigh escaped her lips. She had never wanted anything so much as she wanted Daniel. Turning the pillow, she laid her head on the cool side and went to sleep, wishing he was lying in the double bed beside her.

CHAPTER THIRTEEN

NEXT day, over breakfast, they chatted like a married couple. Edie beamed at their empty plates.

'Will you be in for lunch, Jenna?' Daniel asked.

'No. I usually take sandwiches and have them at the Health Centre.' She did not think she could cope with lunch as well as dinner in his company. Seeing him freshly shaven at breakfast had almost been her undoing. She had found it difficult to speak at all.

'See you at coffee-time, then,' he said as they parted outside.

Jenna smiled and nodded as she climbed into her car. They arrived at the Health Centre within minutes of each other. Daniel was already out of his car and opened her door for her.

'I could get used to this,' she quipped.

'Could you?' It was spoken softly. He had his hand out to assist her.

Not trusting herself, she put her bag into it, and received a raised eyebrow in return. 'Thanks,' she said with a smile.

'I do have my uses,' he grinned, and winked.

'I don't doubt it.' Her smile was as big as his. She could not believe he was being so light-hearted with her, instead of his usual tenseness.

He laughed. They were still laughing as they went into the Health Centre.

Penny was at Reception, and she glared at Jenna. She did not wait for her. Jenna collected her messages from Shirley. One was from a patient informing Jenna that her daughter was coming to stay and would bath her. The other was from Alice Hayes. 'Please phone,' it said.

171

'Can I use one of your phones?' Jenna asked Shirley.

'Sure.' Shirley gestured to the one on the desk.

Jenna dialled. 'Hello, Mrs Hayes,' she said when it was answered. 'What can I do for you?'

'You can come back as my nurse.' Alice's voice was disgruntled. 'I could suffer Miss Brown on your days off, but I can't cope with her every day. She's not as thorough as you are. She doesn't put cream on my ears, and they're sore.'

'I'm sure it's just a matter of you both getting to know each other.' Jenna tried to appease her.

'Well, you tell her about my ears, then.'

'I will,' said Jenna more cheerfully than she felt. It was going to be awkward. Penny was not pleased with her already.

As soon as Jenna entered their room, Penny attacked.

'I thought you said your relationship with Daniel was platonic. You seemed to be pretty chummy when you came in this morning.'

'Well, I can't exactly be rude to him.' Jenna raised her eyebrows.

'You're deliberately trying to get him for yourself!' Penny's face was flushed with anger. 'You're in love with him—admit it!'

Jenna was fed up by this time. Alice Hayes's complaint and Penny's attack on top of Jenna's worry about deceiving Daniel was too much.

'Yes,' she snapped, 'you're quite right—I *am* in love with Daniel, and I mean to have him.' What a relief to speak it out!

Penny was stunned, and Jenna took advantage of this to say, 'Alice Hayes left a message for me to phone her. She wants you to cream her ears.'

Penny burst into tears. 'You've taken Daniel and now you're taking the patients!' She slammed her visiting list down, her eyes anguished. 'I hate you! You can do the lot!' and she rushed for the door.

'Don't be silly, Penny.' Jenna caught up with her, but Penny wrenched the door open and fled from the room before Jenna could grasp her arm. Penny was past Reception and out of the main door before Jenna could catch her.

There was a screech of brakes and a thud. Jenna was held immobile with shock when she saw Penny lying motionless on the tarmac.

'She just ran straight into me,' the shocked driver was saying.

His words broke through Jenna's horror, and she hurried forward. Penny was unconscious, but breathing.

A couple of patients who were coming to the Health Centre stood gaping down at Penny. 'That's the nurse,' one of them said.

'Yes, the fair one,' the other agreed in a whisper.

'The ambulance is coming.' Daniel appeared beside Jenna. His face was as white as hers. He bent to examine Penny. 'No broken bones that I can see.'

Jenna was grateful for his calmness. She was stricken with guilt.

'It was my fault,' she said in a whisper.

Daniel gave her a sharp look. 'What do you mean?' He frowned. 'Oh, never mind that now—fetch a blanket.' His order was direct, delivered in an authoritative tone, and Jenna reacted immediately.

She was back with the blanket in a few moments and was placing it over Penny's inert form when the ambulance arrived. A car was parked in the space reserved for it, so the driver had to stop further away from Penny.

The ambulance men were out with the stretcher and hurrying towards the prostrate figure as Jenna looked up.

'Stand aside—we'll deal with this now,' a grey-haired ambulanceman said. Then he recognised Daniel. 'Oh, sorry Doctor.'

Daniel stood aside. 'She's all yours.' His face was drawn with concern.

They soon had Penny on the stretcher. She did not look like the friend Jenna knew. A graze down her right cheek had altered her appearance, and her face had that deathlike pallor associated with shock. She looked like a stranger.

Jenna's heart was beating so fast that she felt as if it had leapt into her throat.

'Pull yourself together.' Daniel's voice seemed to come from a long way off. 'You'll have to go with her.' His face was close to hers, his hands were on her shoulders, but it was not Daniel's face she saw. It was the grazed, unconscious face of her friend.

His words did, however, penetrate her shock.

'But the patients. . .?' she began.

'I'll phone the nursing officer and tell her what's happened. You must go with Penny now.' His voice was firm. 'They'll need to contact her parents.'

Daniel's mention of Penny's parents made Jenna feel even worse. What was she to say to them? The starting up of the ambulance's engine roused her. She pushed her distress aside and without looking at Daniel went quickly to the driver's side. 'I'll go with you,' she said.

The journey to Swansford General took longer because of the commuter traffic. The paramedic was monitoring Penny's condition. There was nothing for Jenna to do except hold her friend's hand.

At the accident and emergency desk, Jenna explained what had happened and gave Penny's details. The sister came up to her.

'We'll contact her parents. Would you like a cup of tea?' Her smile was kind.

'No, thanks.' Jenna tried to smile, but could not quite make it. 'I'd better get back to work.'

Jenna always carried small change in her pocket in case she had to make an emergency call. She drew out some coins and dialled the senior nursing officer's number and told her that Penny was being admitted to Intensive Care.

'I've arranged for Sarah Armstrong to take Penny's place. She'll be doing the diabetics by now and will be back at the Health Centre by the time you arrive,' the SNO told her.

Jenna thanked her, and, as she replaced the receiver, felt she should phone Charlie. Reluctantly she dialled his number.

'It's Jenna,' she said when he replied.

'What do *you* want?' His tone was not encouraging.

'There's been an accident.' She told him about Penny. 'I'm phoning from the hospital now.'

There was no reply and Jenna thought the line had been cut. 'Are you all right?' she asked.

'How did it happen?' he whispered.

If Jenna had not still been in a state of shock she would never have blurted it out, but she did. She told him about the quarrel and the reason for it. Immediately she regretted her words, but it was too late.

'You bitch!' Charlie shouted. Jenna had to hold the receiver away from her ear. 'It's all your fault! You——' She could not take any more and put the receiver down.

It was an older Jenna who stepped from the bus outside the Health Centre, an older Jenna who answered enquiries about Penny and spoke to the police. She avoided Daniel, who was in surgery, by quickly giving Sarah Penny's work and going out to do her own.

Jenna did not go back for coffee, just phoned to see if there were any messages, saying she was too busy to come in, which was true.

By the time she returned for lunch the doctors had gone. Daniel had left word for her to contact him, but as she took the slip of paper from the receptionist, Linda told her that Daniel had been called out on an emergency. Jenna was glad. She phoned the hospital and was told Penny was still unconscious.

At breakfast that morning Daniel had told Jenna that he was attending a GPs' meeting that afternoon, so she wouldn't have to see him then.

By the time she had finished work, Jenna was so fraught with anxiety that she decided she could not face Daniel at all and phoned Edie to tell her that a friend she had not seen for ages had asked her to spend the night, and did not even bother that it was a lie. What was one more guilt?

She went to the cashline, drew out some money and bought herself a nightdress and toothbrush. Robert's flat was as she had left it. She found a pair of jeans and a jumper lying on her bed and remembered, now, that she had left them in the airing cupboard.

She switched on the fire and the light. She had bought herself some bread, butter, tea and sugar, so she made herself some tea and toast. She wasn't hungry, but her thirst was enormous.

She had drunk two cups of tea and was pouring a third when the bell went. It must be Robert, she thought, and it was not until she had opened the door to find Charlie glowering at her that she realised Robert would have had a key.

Charlie was a big man with a big hand, which he used to thrust her back into the flat. 'I'm going to teach you a lesson!' His face was menacing and ugly, so white that it made his red hair seem brighter. His hand jabbed her chest each time he spoke a word.

Then he started to hit her. She tried to fight, and reached for the vase that stood on the hall table, but it was not there. She clawed for his face, but her nails, kept short for work, made no impression. She was not frightened, she was furious, and she kicked and hit out, but he was too strong, and she fell to the floor under his blows, unable to move. He was kicking her ribs when she lost consciousness.

CHAPTER FOURTEEN

A BANGING noise roused her. It sounded as if it was in her head. Then she thought she heard, from a long way off, Daniel's voice calling impatiently,

'Jenna, answer the door! I know you're in there.'

It took a while for her to realise that it was really him, but her body was so painful that all she wanted to do was to slip back into the security of unconsciousness. The pain would not let her.

'Daniel!' she called, but her face was so swollen, her voice so faint, that she knew he would not be able to hear her, and tears of frustration fell on to her bruised cheeks.

'Come on Jenna!' His impatience was stronger. 'I'm not leaving here until you answer.'

Slowly, painfully, each breath an agony, Jenna dragged herself nearer the door, but she was unable to reach it.

'Daniel—Daniel.' She could taste her tears as they ran into her mouth.

Then she heard the letterbox lift. It was something she had done so many times—at Mrs Dickens', for one—at a patient's house.

'My God!' Daniel's shocked voice came through the letterbox. The next moment the door burst open. 'Jenna darling!'

Had she heard the endearment. Or was it her dazed state making her hallucinate?

'Who did this?' He reached for the phone. 'Don't try to talk. I'll get an ambulance.' Rapidly he gave his name and stated his request.

Jenna's eyelids were swollen and she could hardly see,

but she felt the duvet placed gently over her cold, cold body, felt light fingers on her pulse, thought she heard murmuring endearments, but that could not be so.

She moaned when the ambulancemen lifted her. Then she felt her hand taken.

'I'm here, Jenna.' Daniel's voice was calm and she relaxed. 'Everything will be all right now.' His confidence reassured her.

She wanted to cry, Nothing will be all right ever again if I can't have you, but she was unable to speak and would not have anyway. Tears of unrequited love ran down her cheeks, and were wiped gently away before they could dampen the pillow.

Daniel stayed with her while the doctor examined her, assisting where necessary. He went up to the ward with her and insisted that she have a room to herself. Jenna could see his fair hair through her haze. She whimpered when he let go of her hand and sighed when he took it again. She winced when they gave her injections, but was grateful for the relief which followed.

The police questioned her immediately after she arrived in the ward, but she would not tell them who had attacked her even if she had been able.

'Now, miss. . . You wouldn't want him to attack someone else, would you?'

Making a painful effort, Jenna mumbled, 'It was a private thing.'

'No more, Officer,' said Daniel, seeing how exhausted just those few words made her. But when they had gone he bent over her and said, 'Who was it, Jenna?'

She could not see the expression on his face because her eyelids were so swollen, but she heard the anger in his voice and shook her head, wishing she hadn't when the pain flashed from side to side.

The dinner Susan and Richard were giving for Robert and Elaine was overshadowed by the attack. Both they and Richard, with Susan, spent the evening at the hospital. Jenna's condition worsened, and Daniel phoned Jenna's parents.

'We'll catch the first flight,' her father said.

Robert and Elaine were reluctant to leave for Canada on Monday, but they could not delay their flight.

'We'll keep in touch,' they promied as Susan and Richard saw them off.

Throughout the days that followed, Daniel sat beside Jenna's bed. Whenever she woke he was there. Whenever she slept he was there. His brother could not move him; the staff could not move him. He slept and ate at her bedside. He felt it was the only way he could atone for not admitting that he loved her.

What did it matter that they were not alike? What did it matter if she disrupted his life—it would be a glorious disruption, one he longed for. And with this admission he suddenly felt free, no longer suppressed. The closed look so often seen by Jenna left his face. It didn't matter about her deceiving him about needing accommodation. She must have had a reason, just as Elaine had. He was the one at fault—too rigid.

Gradually Jenna's condition improved. Finding Daniel at her bedside helped. Her parents' arrival brought tears to her eyes. How she had missed them!

'We're staying with Daniel, darling,' her mother told her, looking better than Jenna had ever seen her.

But with their arrival, Daniel's visits became fewer and Jenna pined for him.

As soon as she became well enough, Jenna asked after Penny, and was told her friend was in the other side-ward.

Edie popped in a week later carrying a Thermos flask.

'Just some soup, home-made chicken. Much better for you than that hospital stuff,' she told her.

The swelling on Jenna's face had subsided, though she still looked like a boxer who had lost the fight. Her nose had been broken and was swollen, as were her lips, which had required stitches. These were now out.

That evening Daniel told her that he might not be in at the wekend. Jenna had to force herself not to beg him to visit her.

'You're to convalesce at my house,' he told her, preparing to go. Jenna's spirits soared, then he spoilt it by saying, 'It will mean you'll be with your parents.'

'Thanks,' she said, hoping her misery did not show in her expression.

When he had left she wondered if that was the only reason he was asking her to his home—duty.

Her depression deepened, so she was glad when a knock at the door was followed by Penny's head.

'Is it all right for me to come in?'

'Yes.' Jenna was delighted to see her friend looking so well. It allayed her sense of guilt.

'I thought I'd come and set your mind at rest.' Penny was still pale and her blue eyes looked enormous in her honed face. She did not smile.

'At rest?' Jenna was puzzled.

'Yes.' Penny's eyes were cold. 'I didn't tell the police that the accident was your fault.'

'My. . .' Jenna was shocked, but not too shocked to reply, 'I didn't ask you to run into that car!'

'But you were the instrument.' Anger made Penny's face flush.

Was she? Jenna became exhausted easily. She was still far from well, but she managed to rouse her spirits sufficiently to say,

'Well, if that's true, I've paid for it.' Tears of weakness gathered in her eyes. 'Your champion exacted a pound of flesh for you.'

'What do you mean?' Penny's brows drew together.

'Who do you think is responsible for my being in this bed?' Jenna asked her.

'Charlie?' Penny stared at her. 'My Charlie?'

'Yes, your Charlie.' It was said wryly.

'You didn't tell the police.' There was no concern for Jenna in Penny's voice, just for Charlie.

'No,' Jenna said wearily.

'Charlie did that for me?'

Jenna was appalled at the admiration in Penny's voice. How she must hate me, she thought. Her depression returned with such force that she felt as if a great weight was pressing on her chest and she found it difficult to breathe.

'He must really love me!' Penny's face shone with happiness. She turned towards the door, murmuring, 'How could I have ever thought I was in love with Daniel?' opened it and went out.

Tears fell on to Jenna's cheeks and fell off them unheeded. 'I can't stay in this place any longer!' she wailed, and with difficulty pushed the bedclothes aside. 'I must go.' Her legs moved as if in slow motion until they hung over the side of the bed.

'Here, here! What's this?' Daniel was at her side in a moment, just in time to catch her in his arms as she fell forward. Talcum powder marked his grey jacket with white patches.

'Oh, Daniel!' Jenna wailed. 'Nobody loves me!' It was the cry of a hurt, vulnerable child. Her face had not fully regained its contours, so that its puffiness made it look more childlike.

Daniel lifted her on to his knee and sat with her as he might a child, rocking her gently. 'I love you, Jenna,' he whispered.

'You're just saying that to comfort me.' Her tears fell on to her white nightdress, making round spots. How could she believe him, and if he *was* telling the truth his love would die when he found she had deceived him about needing a place to stay.

'Penny hates me.' Jenna was becoming more distressed by thoughts of Daniel, otherwise she would not

have said, 'She was glad Charlie attacked me.' Her voice
was rising. 'She said I was to blame for her accident,
but it's not true. I only agreed with her when she
accused me of being in love with you—she wanted you
for herself. That's why she ran out of the Health Centre.
It wasn't my fault, was it, Daniel? Tell me it wasn't!'
She was clutching his jacket lapels in her distress.

Daniel was trying to control his anger at hearing that
Charlie was Jenna's attacker, and it showed in his eyes,
but Jenna misread the reason and thought he was angry
with her.

'You do blame me!' she wailed, pushing him away.
'Well, you might as well know it all.' She drew in a
breath and winced. It still hurt. 'I didn't need a room—
Robert had leased me the flat. I only told you that so
that I could be near you in the hope that you'd come to
love me.'

Daniel took her face very gently in both his hands and
kissed her swollen lips. 'Shh, my darling!' Her distress
was his distress, and he hurried to alleviate it. 'I know
about the flat and I don't care. You brought warmth
into my house and into my life. Before, it was a house,
bricks and mortar, but your coming made it a home.'

'But you're angry with me?' The words trembled, but
the tears had stopped.

He put a finger on her lips. 'Hush, my darling!' He
wiped her wet cheeks with his finger. 'I'm not angry
with you—it's Charlie I'm furious with. I'd like to break
his neck! The police——'

It was Jenna's turn to place her finger over his lips.

'No,' she said, calmer now. 'Penny knows it's Charlie
she loves. She'll go back to him, tell him she loves him
and it will all be forgotten.' The sadness was still in her
face.

'Not by me it won't.' Daniel's eyes were grim. His
arms tightened around her, momentarily forgetting her
broken ribs. Jenna winced.

'Oh, I'm sorry, darling.' His face was contrite. Jenna would gladly have had him hug her again just to hear the endearment. She still could not believe he loved her.

'How can you love me when I look like this? I don't even look like me.' She started to tremble.

'Let's put you back to bed.' His eyes were concerned. 'You're cold.'

'No.' Jenna snuggled against him. 'It's my spirit that's cold, not me.'

She sounded so pathetic that he held her close again. He felt like weeping himself, and his hatred for Charlie included Penny. To see his vibrant, courageous Jenna reduced to this sad, tearful woman grieved him more than he would have thought possible. She roused emotions in him he did not know he possessed. It was only now, with her head on his shoulder and her soft hair touching his cheek, that he realised how sterile his life had been before.

Jenna looked up into his face and saw the gentle kindness he bestowed on the patients in his eyes, but there was something else as well. Something that filled her heart with joy. It was love for her in their depth. He did not need to say, 'I shall love you in sickness and in health, and that means when you're bruised and battered in body and mind,' for her to know it was the truth.

He grinned and she smiled. She reached an arm up to encircle his neck and raised herself to touch his lips with hers. Feeling his passion rise, he said, 'I think it's time we put you back in bed,' and winked.

She hated him removing his arms from around her, just as she could see his reluctance to do so. He pulled the bedclothes up to her chin and gave a great sigh of contentment. He didn't see her bruises. He saw the vibrant, alluring Jenna he had first met and knew he had fallen in love with her then.

He bent over her and kissed her bruised eyelids, her cheeks, her lips. 'I don't want to go,' he whispered.

'I don't want you to.' Her voice was as soft as his.

The door opened and the night nurse came in. 'Oh, sorry,' she said. 'I didn't know you were here.'

'Just another minute, Nurse, please,' he said.

She smiled and closed the door behind her.

'Why did you come back?' asked Jenna.

'I came to tell you that you can come home tomorrow.' Daniel smiled. 'I spoke to Nick.' Jenna knew the registrar who was looking after her was a friend of Daniel's. 'He said I can take you home as long as there's someone in constant attendance.' He smiled mischievously. 'I asked him if I would do, and he agreed.' He was sitting on the bed and took hold of Jenna's hands. 'I'm taking a week's leave.' He grinned. 'I want to supervise your convalescence personally.'

Home—what a wonderful word, especially when it was Daniel's home. Jenna smiled. 'My own private doctor!'

'Your own doctor, yes, but not such a private one now.' The clear-cut lines of his face softened. 'You've liberated me, my darling. Set me free from bonds of my own making.' He leaned forward and kissed her gently on the lips.

She touched his face—his dear, beloved face. 'I love you,' she whispered. 'I've loved you from the first moment I saw you.'

Daniel took her into his arms. 'And I you, but I wouldn't admit it.'

There was a knock on the door. 'That'll be the nurse.' He released her reluctantly. 'Come in!' He bent and kissed Jenna on the forehead. 'I'll be here at ten tomorrow morning.'

'I'll be ready,' she smiled up at him.

'You're a very lucky girl,' said the nurse, popping the thermometer into Jenna's mouth. 'Your doctor never left your side day or night until your parents came.'

Jenna could hear the envy in her voice. Knowing this swept away any doubts still lingering.

Next day Daniel arrived before ten. 'I dissuaded your parents from coming—said it would be too exciting for you,' he grinned.

He put a bag with her clothes in on the bed. 'Would you like me to help you to dress? he asked, a cheeky expression on his face.

She smiled. 'No, thanks, I can manage.'

'Would you like the nurse?' It was said gently.

'Well, perhaps.' Jenna did not think she would be able to fasten her bra.

Daniel left, and a junior nurse came in. 'The doctor's gone for the wheelchair,' she said.

Jenna was embrrassed. 'I don't think I need that,' she protested.

But when she rose to dress, her legs felt wobbly. By the time Daniel returned Jenna was feeling quite exhausted. Before she knew what was happening, Daniel swept her up into his arms, but did not immediately place her in the chair.

'I didn't know it was possible to love someone so much that it hurt.' His eyes were serious.

Jenna kissed his cheek, then the other one. His lips met hers in a gentle kiss. 'It's a good job the nurse has left,' he said, grinning.

Edie made more of a fuss of Jenna than her parents when Daniel carried Jenna from the car into the lounge.

'Shouldn't Miss Jenna be in bed? I've put the blanket on.'

'Later,' said Daniel with a smile. 'I think a cup of coffee with her parents first would be nice.'

It took Jenna until Christmas to recover from Charlie's attack, and during that time Daniel was in constant attendance.

Four days after he had brought her home, her parents

were dining at Susan's, leaving Daniel and Jenna alone. He had been very strict about her staying in bed in the mornings, allowing her up at three o'clock, but dispatching her back to bed at eight.

But this evening he had said that she might stay up longer. They were alone. Edie was busy in the kitchen.

'Do you want to see a film?' asked Jenna. The room was warm and she felt sleepy.

Daniel rose to replenish the fire. 'No,' he said.

He stood up and leant his arm on the mantelpiece and, looking down at her, was pleased to see that the bruises and swelling had left her face, but was saddened to see the strain still lingering in her eyes. It would take time and a lot of loving to erase the horror of her attack.

'As your doctor, I prescribe a constant companion.' He smiled.

'Like a dog?' she grinned up at him, noting how the firelight touched his fair hair.

'No.' His eyes were very gentle. Jenna was sitting in the armchair close to the fire. The light from the table lamp fell on her dark hair and olive skin. She was wearing a deep red cashmere sweater that outlined her figure. The unusualness of her beauty quickened his pulse.

He took her hand and pulled her to her feet and into his arms. 'Not like a dog, like a man—this man.' His voice was soft. 'Will you marry me, Jenna?'

Jenna wanted to prolong the delicious moment, so she said, 'Am I to marry the doctor or the man?' smiling impishly into his face.

'Both.' He grinned.

'But that's two men,' she teased. 'I don't know if I could cope with two.'

'Oh, I think you'll manage,' he said, then added wistfully, 'Will you, Jenna? Take us both on?'

For answer, she flung her arms round his neck and

kissed him. 'I wouldn't want to live without you.' There was a catch in her voice. Then she smiled. 'Both of you!'

Daniel kissed her gently and felt her body tremble in his arms as he knew she must feel the tremor in his own. 'It won't be long now,' he whispered, then smiled. 'What do you think of a Christmas wedding? The family will all be here, and it would save your parents having to come over again.'

'Lovely!' Her eyes were bright with happiness.

They sat side by side on the couch, their arms about each other. 'Daniel?' She looked up at him tentatively.

'What is it, my sweet?' He was concerned to see the worry lines back in her face.

'I think perhaps I'd better tell you I'm a virgin.' It came out in a rush, and she blushed.

Daniel stroked her cheek. 'I did wonder when you objected to my telling you to have a smear, but at that time. . .' He looked a bit embarrassed. 'I'm ashamed to say I couldn't believe it.' He smoothed the hair from her face. 'It was too incredible that someone as beautiful and desirable as you should have remained untouched.'

Jenna rested her blushing face against his shoulder.

'I thought I'd better mention it,' she whispered.

'I think I might have found out,' he said.

Jenna glanced up into his grinning face and laughed. Her embarrassment left her and she knew with a wonderful certainty that here was a man who would treat her confidences with respect and love her all the more.

'Christmas seems a long way off,' she whispered.

'Oh, but think of the Christmas present we'll give each other,' Daniel grinned, and kissed her very thoroughly.

Jenna and Daniel were married two days before Christmas, with all their family present.

Their wedding night was spent at his house. Daniel had suggested booking Swansford's best hotel, but

Jenna had said, 'I love your house. It has such an air of peace and happiness.' Then she laughed. 'But I don't think we should include Edie!'

He had laughed and arranged for Edie to visit her sister, all expenses paid.

The scent of chrysanthemums met them as Daniel carried Jenna over the threshold. Pots of them brightened the lounge. A note from Susan wishing them every happiness was propped in front of a bottle of champagne.

'How lovely,' said Jenna, looking up at him, the note still in her hand.

Daniel gathered her into his arms. 'Yes, indeed. How lovely!'

Jenna knew he meant herself, and tears of happiness filled her eyes. She was too overwhelmed to speak. Reaching up, she put her arms round his neck and pulled his face close to hers and kissed him. The kiss bound them together, and without another word they went up to his bedroom. There on the bed lay her umbrella.

'You returned it!' she said, and they both laughed. It relieved their tension.

'But of course. I said I would, didn't I? And I always keep my word.'

'Always?'

Daniel lifted her into his arms and laid her on the bed. He sat beside her as he had sat so often in the hospital.

'Always.' His voice was soft and gentle. 'I'll love you always, and that's a promise.'

Jenna reached up for him.

Their lovemaking was unhurried and gentle, but during the night, after he had initiated her into the ways of love, her passionate nature responded until he was no longer the teacher and came to know a fulfilment he had thought impossible. Jenna had released his inhibitions. It was as if she had cut the band around his heart.

They woke in each other's arms. It was cold and silent, too early for the milkman, too early for the cars.

'If we could stay like this forever,' whispered Jenna.

'You'll feel my arms around you no matter where you are, my lovely Jenna. When you're shopping, when you're working, they'll be there, keeping you safe.'

Jenna knew that would be so. They were part of each other now. They had started something that would never end, and she sighed happily.

'Is that a promise?' she asked cheekily.

'Of course. I always keep my promises, remember?' Then he said with a catch in his voice. 'Till the end of time.'

He kissed her, and, of course, that wasn't the end, just the beginning.

Mills & Boon have commissioned four of your favourite authors to write four tender romances.

Guaranteed love and excitement for St. Valentine's Day

A BRILLIANT DISGUISE	-	Rosalie Ash
FLOATING ON AIR	-	Angela Devine
THE PROPOSAL	-	Betty Neels
VIOLETS ARE BLUE	-	Jennifer Taylor

Available from January 1993   PRICE £3.99

Available from Boots, Martins, John Menzies, W.H. Smith, most supermarkets and other paperback stockists. Also available from Mills & Boon Reader Service, PO Box 236, Thornton Road, Croydon, Surrey CR9 3RU.